Roister Doister

by Nicholas Udall

Dramatis Personæ.

Ralph Roister Doister.

Mathew Merygreeke.

Gawyn Goodluck, *affianced to Dame Custance.*

Tristram Trustie, *his friend.*

Dobinet Doughtie, *'boy' to Roister Doister.*

Tom Trupenie, *seruant to Dame Custance.*

Sym Suresby, *seruant to Goodluck.*

Scriuener.

Harpax.
Dame Christian Custance, *a widow.*

Margerie Mumblecrust, *her nurse.*
Tibet Talk apace,
       her maidens.
Annot Alyface,
Time. *About Two days.*

Scene. *Not indicated: ? London.*

The Prologue.

Hat Creature is in health, eyther yong or olde,
But som mirth with modestie wil be glad to vse
As we in thys Enterlude shall now vnfolde,
Wherin all scurilitie we vtterly refuse,
Auoiding such mirth wherin is abuse:
Knowing nothing more comendable for a mans recreation
Than Mirth which is vsed in an honest fashion:
For Myrth prolongeth lyfe, and causeth health.
Mirth recreates our spirites and voydeth pensiuenesse,
Mirth increaseth amitie, not hindring our wealth,
Mirth is to be vsed both of more and lesse,
Being mixed with vertue in decent comlynesse.
As we trust no good nature can gainsay the same:
Which mirth we intende to vse, auoidyng all blame.
The wyse Poets long time heretofore,
Vnder merrie Comedies secretes did declare,
Wherein was contained very vertuous lore,
With mysteries and forewarnings very rare.
Suche to write neither *Plautus* nor *Terence* dyd spare,
Whiche among the learned at this day beares the bell:
These with such other therein dyd excell.
Our Comedie or Enterlude which we intende to play.
Is named Royster Doyster in deede.
Which against the vayne glorious doth inuey,
Whose humour the roysting sort continually doth feede.
Thus by your pacience we intende to proceede
In this our Enterlude by Gods leaue and grace,
And here I take my leaue for a certaine space.
FINIS.

11
Roister Doister.

Actus. j. Scæna. j.
Mathewe Merygreeke. He entreth singing.

S long lyueth the mery man (they say)
As doth the sory man, and longer by a day.
Yet the Grassehopper for all his Sommer pipyng,
Sterueth in Winter wyth hungrie gripyng,
Therefore an other sayd sawe doth men aduise,
That they be together both mery and wise.
Thys Lesson must I practise, or else ere long,
Wyth mee Mathew Merygreeke it will be wrong.
In deede men so call me, for by him that vs bought,
What euer chaunce betide, I can take no thought,
Yet wisedome woulde that I did my selfe bethinke
Where to be prouided this day of meate and drinke:
For know ye, that for all this merie note of mine,
He might appose me now that should aske where I dine.
My lyuing lieth heere and there, of Gods grace,
Sometime wyth this good man, sometyme in that place,
Sometime Lewis Loytrer biddeth me come neere,
Somewhyles Watkin Waster maketh vs good cheere,
Sometime Dauy Diceplayer when he hath well cast
Keepeth reuell route as long as it will last.
Sometime Tom Titiuile maketh vs a feast,
Sometime with sir Hugh Pye I am a bidden gueast,
Sometime at Nichol Neuerthriues I get a soppe,
Sometime I am feasted with Bryan Blinkinsoppe,
Sometime I hang on Hankin Hoddydodies sleeue,
But thys day on Ralph Royster Doysters by hys leeue.
For truely of all men he is my chiefe banker
Both for meate and money, and my chiefe shootanker.
12
For, sooth Roister Doister in that he doth say,
And require what ye will ye shall haue no nay.
But now of Roister Doister somewhat to expresse,

That ye may esteeme him after hys worthinesse,
In these twentie townes and seke them throughout,
Is not the like stocke, whereon to graffe a loute.
All the day long is he facing and craking
Of his great actes in fighting and fraymaking:
But when Roister Doister is put to his proofe,
To keepe the Queenes peace is more for his behoofe.
If any woman smyle or cast on hym an eye,
Vp is he to the harde eares in loue by and by,
And in all the hotte haste must she be hys wife.
Else farewell hys good days, and farewell his life,
Maister Raufe Royster Doister is but dead and gon
Excepte she on hym take some compassion,
Then chiefe of counsell, must be Mathew Merygreeke,
What if I for mariage to suche an one seeke?
Then must I sooth it, what euer it is:
For what he sayth or doth can not be amisse,
Holde vp his yea and nay, be his nowne white sonne,
Prayse and rouse him well, and ye haue his heart wonne,
For so well liketh he his owne fonde fashions
That he taketh pride of false commendations.
But such sporte haue I with him as I would not leese,
Though I should be bounde to lyue with bread and cheese.
For exalt hym, and haue hym as ye lust in deede:
Yea to hold his finger in a hole for a neede.
I can with a worde make him fayne or loth,
I can with as much make him pleased or wroth,
I can when I will make him mery and glad,
I can when me lust make him sory and sad,
I can set him in hope and eke in dispaire,
I can make him speake rough, and make him speake faire.
But I maruell I see hym not all thys same day,
I wyll seeke him out: But loe he commeth thys way,
I haue yond espied hym sadly comming,

And in loue for twentie pounde, by hys glommyng.

13

Actus. j. Scæna. ij.

Rafe Roister Doister. Mathew Merygreeke.

R. Royster.

Ome death when thou wilt, I am weary of my life.

M. Mery. I tolde you I, we should wowe another wife.

R. Royster. Why did God make me suche a goodly person?

M. Mery. He is in by the weke, we shall haue sport anon.

R. Royster. And where is my trustie friende Mathew Merygreeke?

M. Mery. I wyll make as I sawe him not, he doth me seeke.

R. Royster. I haue hym espyed me thinketh, yond is hee,

Hough Mathew Merygreeke my friend, a worde with thee.

M. Mery. I wyll not heare him, but make as I had haste,

Farewell all my good friendes, the tyme away dothe waste,

And the tide they say, tarieth for no man.

R. Royster. Thou must with thy good counsell helpe me if thou can.

M. Mery. God keepe thee worshypfull Maister Roister Doister,

And fare well the lustie Maister Roister Doister.

R. Royster. I muste needes speake with thee a worde or twaine.

M. Mery. Within a month or two I will be here againe,

Negligence in greate affaires ye knowe may marre all.

R. Royster. Attende vpon me now, and well rewarde thee I shall.

M. Mery. I haue take my leaue, and the tide is well spent.

R. Royster. I die except thou helpe, I pray thee be content,

Doe thy parte wel nowe, and aske what thou wilt,

14

For without thy aide my matter is all spilt.

M. Mery. Then to serue your turne I will some paines take,

And let all myne owne affaires alone for your sake.

R. Royster. My whole hope and trust resteth onely in thee.

M. Mery. Then can ye not doe amisse what euer it bee.

R. Royster. Gramercies Merygreeke, most bounde to thee I am.

M. Mery. But vp with that heart, and speake out like a ramme,

Ye speake like a Capon that had the cough now:

Bee of good cheere, anon ye shall doe well ynow.

R. Royster. Vpon thy comforte, I will all things well handle.

M. Mery. So loe, that is a breast to blowe out a candle.

But what is this great matter I woulde faine knowe,

We shall fynde remedie therefore I trowe.

Doe ye lacke money? ye knowe myne olde offers,

Ye haue always a key to my purse and coffers.

R. Royster. I thanke thee: had euer man suche a frende?

M. Mery. Ye gyue vnto me: I must needes to you lende.

R. Royster. Nay I haue money plentie all things to discharge.

M. Mery. That knewe I ryght well when I made offer so large.

But it is no suche matter.

A handwritten note in the margin gives the previous half-line to "R. Royster". This is probably correct.

M. Mery. What is it than?

Are ye in daunger of debte to any man?

If ye be, take no thought nor be not afraide,

Let them hardly take thought how they shall be paide.

R. Royster. Tut I owe nought.

M. Mery. What then? fear ye imprisonment?

R. Royster. No.

M. Mery. No I wist ye offende, not so to be shent.

But if he had, the Toure coulde not you so holde,

But to breake out at all times ye would be bolde.

What is it? hath any man threatned you to beate?

R. Royster. What is he that durst haue put me in that heate?

15

He that beateth me by his armes shall well fynde,

That I will not be farre from him nor runne behinde.

M. Mery. That thing knowe all men euer since ye ouerthrewe,

The fellow of the Lion which *Hercules* slewe.

But what is it than?

R. Royster. Of loue I make my mone.

M. Mery. Ah this foolishe a loue, wilt neare let vs alone?

But bicause ye were refused the last day,

Ye sayd ye woulde nere more be intangled that way.

I woulde medle no more, since I fynde all so vnkinde.

R. Royster. Yea, but I can not so put loue out of my minde.

Math. Mer. But is your loue tell me first, in any wise,

In the way of Mariage, or of Merchandise?

If it may otherwise than lawfull be founde,

Ye get none of my helpe for an hundred pounde.

R. Royster. No by my trouth I woulde haue hir to my Wife.

M. Mery. Then are ye a good man, and God saue your life,

And what or who is she, with whome ye are in loue?

R. Royster. A woman whome I knowe not by what meanes to moue.

M. Mery. Who is it?

R. Royster. A woman yond.

M. Mery. What is hir name?

R. Royster. Hir yonder.

M. Mery. Whom.

R. Royster. Mistresse ah.

M. Mery. Fy fy for shame

Loue ye, and know not whome? but hir yonde, a Woman,

We shall then get you a Wyfe, I can not tell whan.

R. Royster. The faire Woman, that supped wyth vs yesternyght,

And I hearde hir name twice or thrice, and had it ryght.

M. Mery. Yea, ye may see ye nere take me to good cheere with you,

If ye had, I coulde haue tolde you hir name now.

R. Royster. I was to blame in deede, but the nexte tyme perchaunce:

And she dwelleth in this house.

M. Mery. What Christian Custance.

R. Royster. Except I haue hir to my Wife, I shall runne madde.

M. Mery. Nay vnwise perhaps, but I warrant you for madde.

R. Royster. I am vtterly dead vnlesse I haue my desire.

M. Mery. Where be the bellowes that blewe this sodeine fire?

R. Royster. I heare she is worthe a thousande pounde and more.

M. Mery. Yea, but learne this one lesson of me afore,

An hundred pounde of Marriage money doubtlesse,

Is euer thirtie pounde sterlyng, or somewhat lesse,

So that hir Thousande pounde yf she be thriftie,

Is muche neere about two hundred and fiftie,

Howebeit wowers and Widowes are neuer poore.

R. Royster. Is she a Widowe? I loue hir better therefore.

M. Mery. But I heare she hath made promise to another.

R. Royster. He shall goe without hir, and he were my brother.

M. Mery. I haue hearde say, I am right well aduised,

That she hath to Gawyn Goodlucke promised.

R. Royster. What is that Gawyn Goodlucke?

M. Mery. a Merchant man.

R. Royster. Shall he speede afore me? nay sir by sweete Sainct Anne.

Ah sir, Backare quod Mortimer to his sowe,

I wyll haue hir myne owne selfe I make God a vow.

For I tell thee, she is worthe a thousande pounde.

M. Mery. Yet a fitter wife for your maship might be founde:

Suche a goodly man as you, might get one wyth lande,

Besides poundes of golde a thousande and a thousande,

And a thousande, and a thousande, and a thousande,

And so to the summe of twentie hundred thousande,

Your most goodly personage is worthie of no lesse.

R. Royster. I am sorie God made me so comely doubtlesse.

17

For that maketh me eche where so highly fauoured,

And all women on me so enamoured.

M. Mery. Enamoured quod you? haue ye spied out that?

Ah sir, mary nowe I see you know what is what.

Enamoured ka? mary sir say that againe,

But I thought not ye had marked it so plaine.

R. Royster. Yes, eche where they gaze all vpon me and stare.

M. Mery. Yea malkyn, I warrant you as muche as they dare.

And ye will not beleue what they say in the streete,

When your mashyp passeth by all such as I meete,

That sometimes I can scarce finde what aunswere to make.

Who is this (sayth one) sir *Launcelot du lake*?

Who is this, greate *Guy* of Warwike, sayth an other?

No (say I) it is the thirtenth *Hercules* brother.

Who is this? noble *Hector* of *Troy*, sayth the thirde?

No, but of the same nest (say I) it is a birde.

Who is this? greate *Goliah*, *Sampson*, or *Colbrande*?

No (say I) but it is a brute of the Alie lande.

Who is this? greate *Alexander*? or *Charle le Maigne*?

No, it is the tenth Worthie, say I to them agayne:

I knowe not if I sayd well.

R. Royster. Yes for so I am.

M. Mery. Yea, for there were but nine worthies before ye came.

To some others, the thirde *Cato* I doe you call.

And so as well as I can I aunswere them all.

Sir I pray you, what lorde or great gentleman is this?

Maister Ralph Roister Doister dame say I, ywis.

O Lorde (sayth she than) what a goodly man it is,

Woulde Christ I had such a husbande as he is.

O Lorde (say some) that the sight of his face we lacke:

It is inough for you (say I) to see his backe.

His face is for ladies of high and noble parages.

With whome he hardly scapeth great mariages.

With muche more than this, and much otherwise.

R. Royster. I can thee thanke that thou canst suche answeres deuise:

But I perceyue thou doste me throughly knowe.

18

M. Mery. I marke your maners for myne owne learnyng I trowe,

But suche is your beautie, and suche are your actes,

Suche is your personage, and suche are your factes,

That all women faire and fowle, more and lesse,

That eye you, they lubbe you, they talke of you doubtlesse,

Your p[l]easant looke maketh them all merie,

Ye passe not by, but they laugh till they be werie,

Yea and money coulde I haue the truthe to tell,

Of many, to bryng you that way where they dwell.

R. Royster. Merygreeke for this thy reporting well of mee:

M. Mery. What shoulde I else sir, it is my duetie pardee:

R. Royster. I promise thou shalt not lacke, while I haue a grote.

M. Mery. Faith sir, and I nere had more nede of a newe cote.

R. Royster. Thou shalte haue one to morowe, and golde for to spende.

M. Mery. Then I trust to bring the day to a good ende.

For as for mine owne parte hauing money inowe,

I could lyue onely with the remembrance of you.

But nowe to your Widowe whome you loue so hotte.

R. Royster. By cocke thou sayest truthe, I had almost forgotte.

M. Mery. What if Christian Custance will not haue you what?

R. Royster. Haue me? yes I warrant you, neuer doubt of that,

I knowe she loueth me, but she dare not speake.

M. Mery. In deede meete it were some body should it breake.

R. Royster. She looked on me twentie tymes yesternight,

And laughed so.

M. Mery. That she coulde not sitte vpright,

R. Royster. No faith coulde she not.

M. Mery. No euen such a thing I cast.

R. Royster. But for wowyng thou knowest women are shamefast.

But and she knewe my minde, I knowe she would be glad,

And thinke it the best chaunce that euer she had.

19

M. Mery. Too hir then like a man, and be bolde forth to starte,

Wowers neuer speede well, that haue a false harte.

R. Royster. What may I best doe?

M. Mery. Sir remaine ye a while,

Ere long one or other of hir house will appere.

Ye knowe my minde.

R. Royster. Yea now hardly lette me alone.

M. Mery. In the meane time sir, if you please, I wyll home,

And call your Musitians, for in this your case

It would sette you forth, and all your wowyng grace,

Ye may not lacke your instrumentes to play and sing.

R. Royster. Thou knowest I can doe that.

M. Mery. As well as any thing.

Shall I go call your folkes, that ye may shewe a cast?

R. Royster. Yea runne I beseeche thee in all possible haste.

M. Mery. I goe. Exeat.

R. Royster. Yea for I loue singyng out of measure,

It comforteth my spirites and doth me great pleasure.

But who commeth forth yond from my swete hearte Custance?

My matter frameth well, thys is a luckie chaunce.

Actus. j. Scæna. iij.

Mage Mumble crust, spinning on the distaffe. Tibet Talk apace, sowyng. Annot Alyface knittyng. R. Roister.

M. Mumbl.

F thys distaffe were spoonne Margerie Mumblecrust.

Tib Talk. Where good stale ale is will drinke no water I trust.

M. Mumbl. Dame Custance hath promised vs good ale and white bread.

Tib Talk. If she kepe not promise, I will beshrewe her head:

20

But it will be starke nyght before I shall haue done.

R. Royster. I will stande here a while, and talke with them anon,

I heare them speake of Custance, which doth my heart good,

To heare hir name spoken doth euen comfort my blood.

M. Mumbl. Sit downe to your worke Tibet like a good girle.

Tib. Talk. Nourse medle you with your spyndle and your whirle,

No haste but good, Madge Mumblecrust, for whip and whurre

The olde prouerbe doth say, neuer made good furre.

M. Mumbl. Well, ye wyll sitte downe to your worke anon, I trust.

Tib. Talk. Soft fire maketh sweete malte, good Madge Mumblecrust.

M. Mumbl. And sweete malte maketh ioly good ale for the nones.

Tib. Talk. Whiche will slide downe the lane without any bones. Cantet.

Olde browne bread crustes must haue much good mumblyng,

But good ale downe your throte hath good easie tumbling.

R. Royster. The iolyest wenche that ere I hearde, little mouse,

May I not reioyce that she shall dwell in my house?

Tib. Talk. So sirrha, nowe this geare beginneth for to frame.

M. Mumbl. Thanks to God, though your work stand stil, your tong is not lame

Tib. Talk. And though your teeth be gone, both so sharpe and so fine

Yet your tongue can renne on patins as well as mine.

M. Mumbl. Ye were not for nought named Tyb Talke apace.

Tib. Talk. Doth my talke grieue you? Alack, God saue your grace.

M. Mumbl. I holde a grote ye will drinke anon for this geare.

21

Tib. Talk. And I wyll pray you the stripes for me to beare.

M. Mumbl. I holde a penny, ye will drink without a cup.

Tib. Talk. Wherein so ere ye drinke, I wote ye drinke all vp.

An. Alyface. By Cock and well sowed, my good Tibet Talke apace.

Tib. Talk. And een as well knitte my nowne Annot Alyface.

R. Royster. See what a sort she kepeth that must be my wife.

Shall not I when I haue hir, leade a merrie life?

Tib. Talk. Welcome my good wenche, and sitte here by me iust.

An. Alyface. And howe doth our old beldame here, Mage Mumblecrust?

Tib. Talk. Chyde, and finde faultes, and threaten to complaine.

An. Alyface. To make vs poore girles shent to hir is small gaine.

M. Mumbl. I dyd neyther chyde, nor complaine, nor threaten.

R. Royster. It woulde grieue my heart to see one of them beaten.

M. Mumbl. I dyd nothyng but byd hir worke and holde hir peace.

Tib. Talk. So would I, if you coulde your clattering ceasse:

But the deuill can not make olde trotte holde hir tong.

An. Alyface. Let all these matters passe, and we three sing a song,

So shall we pleasantly bothe the tyme beguile now,

And eke dispatche all our workes ere we can tell how.

Tib. Talk. I shrew them that say nay, and that shall not be I.

M. Mumbl. And I am well content.

Tib. Talk. Sing on then by and by.

R. Royster. And I will not away, but listen to their song,

Yet Merygreeke and my folkes tary very long.

22

Tib, An, and Margerie, doe singe here.

Pipe mery Annot. etc.

Trilla, Trilla. Trillarie.

Worke Tibet, worke Annot, worke Margerie.

Sewe Tibet, knitte Annot, spinne Margerie.

Let vs see who shall winne the victorie.

Tib. Talk. This sleue is not willyng to be sewed I trowe,

A small thing might make me all in the grounde to throwe.

Then they sing agayne.

Pipe merrie Annot. etc.

Trilla. Trilla. Trillarie.

What Tibet, what Annot, what Margerie.

Ye sleepe, but we doe not, that shall we trie.

Your fingers be nombde, our worke will not lie.

Tib. Talk. If ye doe so againe, well I would aduise you nay.

In good sooth one stoppe more, and I make holy day.

They singe the thirde tyme.

Pipe Mery Annot. etc.

Trilla. Trilla. Trillarie.

Nowe Tibbet, now Annot, nowe Margerie.

Nowe whippet apace for the maystrie,

But it will not be, our mouth is so drie.

Tib. Talk. Ah, eche finger is a thombe to day me thinke,

I care not to let all alone, choose it swimme or sinke.

They sing the fourth tyme.

Pipe Mery Annot. etc.

Trilla. Trilla. Trillarie.

When Tibet, when Annot, when Margerie.

I will not, I can not, no more can I. Lette hir caste downe hir vvorke.

Then giue we all ouer, and there let it lye.

Tib. Talk. There it lieth, the worste is but a curried cote,

23

Tut I am vsed therto, I care not a grote.

An. Alyface. Haue we done singyng since? then will I in againe,

Here I founde you, and here I leaue both twaine. Exeat.

M. Mumbl. And I will not be long after: Tib Talke apace.

Tib. Talk. What is ye matter?

M. Mumb. Yond stode a man al this space

And hath hearde all that euer we spake togyther.

Tib. Talk. Mary the more loute he for his comming hither.

And the lesse good he can to listen maidens talke.

I care not and I go byd him hence for to walke:

It were well done to knowe what he maketh here away.

R. Royster. Nowe myght I speake to them, if I wist what to say.

M. Mumbl. Nay we will go both off, and see what he is.

R. Royster. One that hath hearde all your talke and singyng ywis.

Tib. Talk. The more to blame you, a good thriftie husbande

Woulde elsewhere haue had some better matters in hande.

R. Royster. I dyd it for no harme, but for good loue I beare,

To your dame mistresse Custance, I did your talke heare.

And Mistresse nource I will kisse you for acquaintance.

M. Mumbl. I come anon sir.

Tib. Talk. Faith I would our dame Custance

21

Sawe this geare.

M. Mumbl. I must first wipe al cleane, yea I must.

Tib. Talk. Ill chieue it dotyng foole, but it must be cust.

M. Mumbl. God yelde you sir, chad not so much ichotte not whan,

Nere since chwas bore chwine, of such a gay gentleman.

R. Royster. I will kisse you too mayden for the good will I beare you.

Tib. Talk. No forsoth, by your leaue ye shall not kisse me.

24

R. Royster. Yes be not afearde, I doe not disdayne you a whit.

Tib. Talk. Why shoulde I feare you? I haue not so little wit,

Ye are but a man I knowe very well.

R. Royster. Why then?

Tib. Talk. Forsooth for I wyll not, I vse not to kisse men.

R. Royster. I would faine kisse you too good maiden, if I myght.

Tib. Talk. What shold that neede?

R. Royster. But to honor you by this light.

I vse to kisse all them that I loue to God I vowe.

Tib. Talk. Yea sir? I pray you when dyd ye last kisse your cowe.

R. Royster. Ye might be proude to kisse me, if ye were wise.

Tib. Talk. What promotion were therein?

R. Royster. Nourse is not so nice.

Tib. Talk. Well I haue not bene taught to kissing and licking.

R. Royster. Yet I thanke you mistresse Nourse, ye made no sticking.

M. Mumbl. I will not sticke for a kosse with such a man as you.

Tib. Talk. They that lust: I will againe to my sewyng now.

An. Alyfac[e]. Tidings hough, tidings, dame Custance greeteth you well.

R. Royster. Whome me?

An. Alyface. You sir? no sir? I do no suche tale tell.

R. Royster. But and she knewe me here.

An. Alyface. Tybet Talke apace,

Your mistresse Custance and mine, must speake with your grace.

Tib. Talk. With me?

An. Alyface. Ye muste come in to hir out of all doutes.

Tib. Talk. And my work not half done? A mischief on all loutes. Ex. am.

25

R. Royster. Ah good sweet nourse.

M. Mumb. A good sweete gentleman.

R. Royster. What?

M. Mumbl. Nay I can not tel sir, but what thing would you?

R. Royster. Howe dothe sweete Custance, my heart of gold, tell me how?

M. Mumbl. She dothe very well sir, and commaunde me to you.

R. Royster. To me?

M. Mumbl. Yea to you sir.

R. Royster. To me? nurse tel me plain

To me?

M. Mumb. Ye.

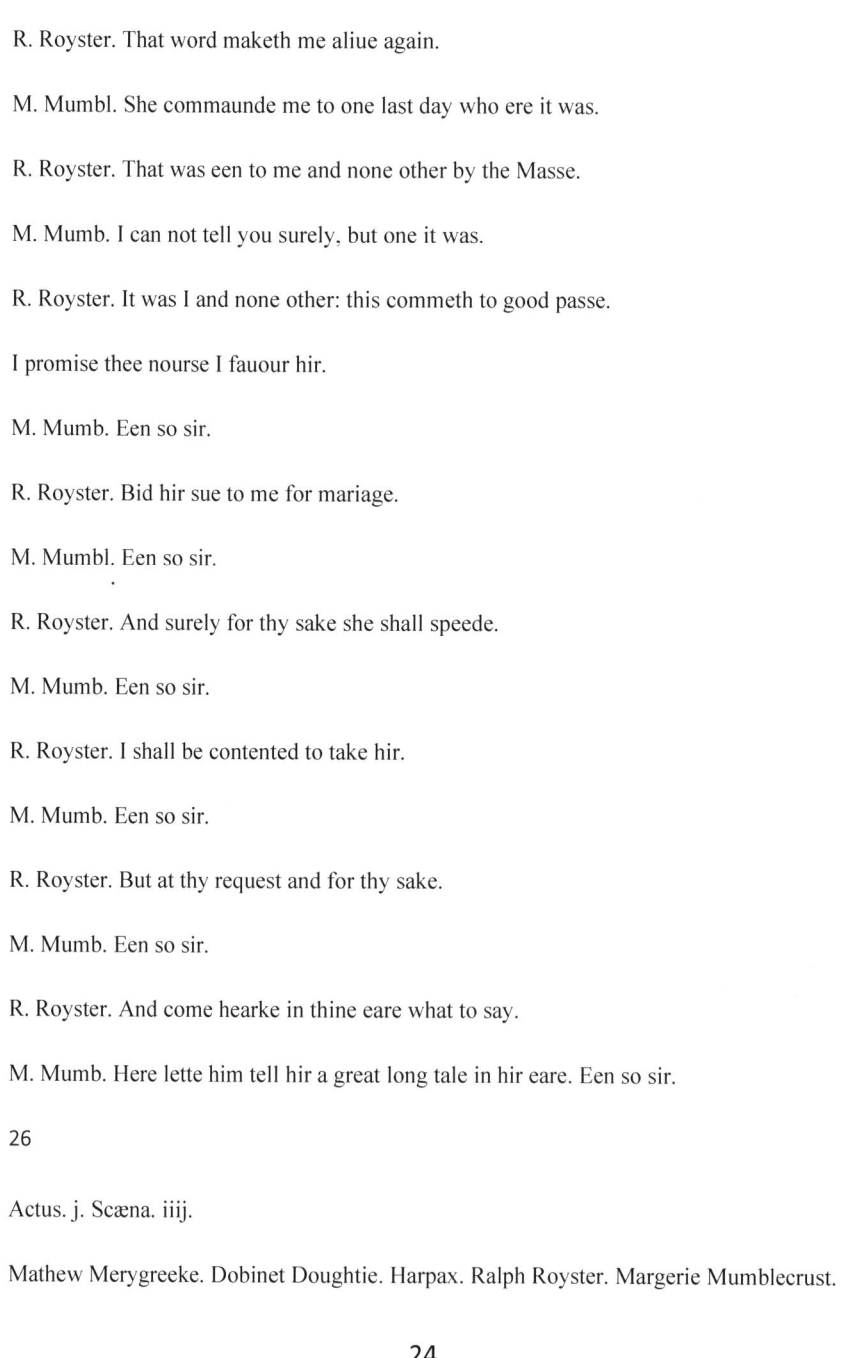

R. Royster. That word maketh me aliue again.

M. Mumbl. She commaunde me to one last day who ere it was.

R. Royster. That was een to me and none other by the Masse.

M. Mumb. I can not tell you surely, but one it was.

R. Royster. It was I and none other: this commeth to good passe.

I promise thee nourse I fauour hir.

M. Mumb. Een so sir.

R. Royster. Bid hir sue to me for mariage.

M. Mumbl. Een so sir.

R. Royster. And surely for thy sake she shall speede.

M. Mumb. Een so sir.

R. Royster. I shall be contented to take hir.

M. Mumb. Een so sir.

R. Royster. But at thy request and for thy sake.

M. Mumb. Een so sir.

R. Royster. And come hearke in thine eare what to say.

M. Mumb. Here lette him tell hir a great long tale in hir eare. Een so sir.

Actus. j. Scæna. iiij.

Mathew Merygreeke. Dobinet Doughtie. Harpax. Ralph Royster. Margerie Mumblecrust.

M. Mery.

Ome on sirs apace, and quite your selues like men,

Your pains shalbe rewarded.

D. Dou. But I wot not when.

M. Mery. Do your maister worship as ye haue done in time past.

D. Dough. Speake to them: of mine office he shall haue a cast.

M. Mery. *Harpax*, looke that thou doe well too, and thy fellow.

Harpax. I warrant, if he will myne example folowe.

M. Mery. Curtsie whooresons, douke you and crouche at euery worde,

D. Dough. Yes whether our maister speake earnest or borde.

M. Mery. For this lieth vpon his preferment in deede.

D. Dough. Oft is hee a wower, but neuer doth he speede.

M. Mery. But with whome is he nowe so sadly roundyng yond?

D. Dough. With *Nobs nicebecetur miserere* sonde.

[M.] Mery. God be at your wedding, be ye spedde alredie?

I did not suppose that your loue was so greedie,

I perceiue nowe ye haue chose of deuotion,

And ioy haue ye ladie of your promotion.

R. Royster. Tushe foole, thou art deceiued, this is not she.

M. Mery. Well mocke muche of hir, and keepe hir well I vise ye.

I will take no charge of such a faire piece keeping.

M. Mumbl. What ayleth thys fellowe? he driueth me to weeping.

M. Mery. What weepe on the weddyng day? be merrie woman,

Though I say it, ye haue chose a good gentleman.

R. Royster. Kocks nownes what meanest thou man, tut a whistle.

27

[M. Mery.] Ah sir, be good to hir, she is but a gristle,

Ah sweete lambe and coney.

R. Royster. Tut thou art deceiued.

M. Mery. Weepe no more lady, ye shall be well receiued.

Vp wyth some mery noyse sirs, to bring home the bride.

R. Royster. Gogs armes knaue, art thou madde?

I tel thee thou art wide.

M. Mery. Then ye entende by nyght to haue hir home brought.

R. Royster. I tel thee no.

M. Mery. How then?

R. Royster. Tis neither ment ne thought.

M. Mery. What shall we then doe with hir?

R. Royster. Ah foolish harebraine,

This is not she.

M. Mery. No is? why then vnsayde againe,

And what yong girle is this with your mashyp so bolde?

R. Royster. A girle?

M. Mery. Yea. I dare say, scarse yet three score yere old.

R. Royster. This same is the faire widowes nourse of whome ye wotte.

M. Mery. Is she but a nourse of a house? hence home olde trotte,

Hence at once.

R. Royster. No, no.

M. Mery. What an please your maship

A nourse talke so homely with one of your worship?

R. Royster. I will haue it so: it is my pleasure and will.

M. Mery. Then I am content. Nourse come againe, tarry still.

R. Royster. What, she will helpe forward this my sute for hir part.

M. Mery. Then ist mine owne pygs nie, and blessing on my hart.

R. Royster. This is our best friend man.

M. Mery. Then teach hir what to say

M. Mumbl. I am taught alreadie.

M. Mery. Then go, make no delay.

R. Royster. Yet hark one word in thine eare.

M. Mery. Back sirs from his taile.

R. Royster. Backe vilaynes, will ye be priuie of my counsaile?

M. Mery. Backe sirs, so: I tolde you afore ye woulde be shent.

R. Royster. She shall haue the first day a whole pecke of argent.

M. Mumbl. A pecke? *Nomine patris*, haue ye so much spare?

R. Royster. Yea and a carte lode therto, or else were it bare,

Besides other mouables, housholde stuffe and lande.

M. Mumbl. Haue ye lands too.

R. Royster. An hundred marks.

M. Mery. Yea a thousand

M. Mumbl. And haue ye cattell too? and sheepe too?

R. Royster. Yea a fewe.

M. Mery. He is ashamed the numbre of them to shewe.

Een rounde about him, as many thousande sheepe goes,

As he and thou and I too, haue fingers and toes.

M. Mumbl. And how many yeares olde be you?

R. Royster. Fortie at lest.

M. Mery. Yea and thrice fortie to them.

R. Royster. Nay now thou dost iest.

I am not so olde, thou misreckonest my yeares.

M. Mery. I know that: but my minde was on bullockes and steeres.

M. Mumbl. And what shall I shewe hir your masterships name is?

R. Royster. Nay she shall make sute ere she know that ywis.

M. Mumbl. Yet let me somewhat knowe.

M. Mery. This is hee vnderstand,

That killed the blewe Spider in Blanchepouder lande.

M. Mumbl. Yea *Iesus*, William zee law, dyd he zo law?

M. Mery. Yea and the last Elephant that euer he sawe,

As the beast passed by, he start out of a buske,

And een with pure strength of armes pluckt out his great tuske.

M. Mumbl. *Iesus, nomine patris*, what a thing was that?

R. Royster. Yea but Merygreke one thing thou hast forgot.

M. Mery. What?

R. Royster. Of thother Elephant.

M. Mery. Oh hym that fledde away.

R. Royster. Yea.

M. Mery. Yea he knew that his match was in place that day

Tut, he bet the king of Crickets on Christmasse day,

That he crept in a hole, and not a worde to say.

M. Mumbl. A sore man by zembletee.

M. Mery. Why, he wrong a club

Once in a fray out of the hande of Belzebub.

R. Roister. And how when Mumfision?

M. Mery. Oh your coustrelyng

Bore the lanterne a fielde so before the gozelyng.

Nay that is to long a matter now to be tolde:

Neuer aske his name Nurse, I warrant thee, be bolde,

He conquered in one day from *Rome*, to *Naples*,

And woonne Townes nourse as fast as thou canst make Apples.

M. Mumbl. O Lorde, my heart quaketh for feare: he is to sore.

R. Roister. Thou makest hir to much afearde, Merygreeke no more.

This tale woulde feare my sweete heart Custance right euill.

M. Mery. Nay let hir take him Nurse, and feare not the deuill.

But thus is our song dasht. Sirs ye may home againe.

R. Roister. No shall they not. I charge you all here to remaine:

The villaine slaues a whole day ere they can be founde.

M. Mery. Couche on your marybones whooresons, down to the ground.

Was it meete he should tarie so long in one place

Without harmonie of Musike, or some solace?

Who so hath suche bees as your maister in hys head,

Had neede to haue his spirites with Musike to be fed.

By your maisterships licence.

R. Roister. What is that? a moate?

M. Mery. No it was a fooles feather had light on your coate.

R. Roister. I was nigh no feathers since I came from my bed.

M. Mery. No sir, it was a haire that was fall from your hed.

R. Roister. My men com when it plese them.

M. Mery. By your leue.

R. Roister. What is that?

M. Mery. Your gown was foule spotted with the foot of a gnat.

R. Roister. Their maister to offende they are nothing afearde.

What now?

30

M. Mery. A lousy haire from your masterships beard.

Omnes famulæ. And sir for Nurses sake pardon this one offence.

We shall not after this shew the like negligence.

R. Royster. I pardon you this once, and come sing nere the wurse.

M. Mery. How like you the goodnesse of this gentleman nurse?

M. Mumbl. God saue his maistership that so can his men forgeue,

And I wyll heare them sing ere I go, by his leaue.

R. Royster. Mary and thou shalt wenche, come we two will daunce.

M. Mumbl. Nay I will by myne owne selfe foote the song perchaunce.

R. Royster. Go to it sirs lustily.

M. Mumbl. Pipe vp a mery note,

Let me heare it playde, I will foote it for a grote.

Cantent.

R. Royster. Now nurse take thys same letter here to thy mistresse.

And as my trust is in thee plie my businesse.

M. Mumbl. It shalbe done?

M. Mery. Who made it?

R. Royster. I wrote it ech whit.

M. Mery. Then nedes it no mending.

R. Royster. No, no.

M. Mery. No I know your wit.

I warrant it wel.

M. Mumbl. It shal be deliuered.

But if ye speede, shall I be considered?

M. Mery. Whough, dost thou doubt of that?

Madge. What shal I haue?

M. Mery. An hundred times more than thou canst deuise to craue.

M. Mumbl. Shall I haue some newe geare? for my olde is all spent.

M. Mery. The worst kitchen wench shall goe in ladies rayment.

M. Mumbl. Yea?

M. Mery. And the worst drudge in the house shal go better

Than your mistresse doth now.

Mar. Then I trudge with your letter.

R. Royster. Now may I repose me: Custance is mine owne.

Let vs sing and play homeward that it may be knowne.

M. Mery. But are you sure, that your letter is well enough?

R. Royster. I wrote it my selfe.

M. Mery. Then sing we to dinner.

Here they sing, and go out singing.

Actus. j. Scæna. v.

Christian Custance. Margerie Mumblecrust.

C. Custance.

Ho tooke thee thys letter Margerie Mumblecrust?

M. Mumbl. A lustie gay bacheler tooke it me of trust,

And if ye seeke to him he will lowe your doing.

C. Custance. Yea, but where learned he that manner of wowing?

M. Mumbl. If to sue to hym, you will any paines take,

He will haue you to his wife (he sayth) for my sake.

C. Custance. Some wise gentleman belike. I am bespoken:

And I thought verily thys had bene some token

From my dere spouse Gawin Goodluck, whom when him please

God luckily sende home to both our heartes ease.

M. Mumbl. A ioyly man it is I wote well by report,

And would haue you to him for marriage resort:

Best open the writing, and see what it doth speake.

C. Custance. At thys time nourse I will neither reade ne breake.

M. Mumbl. He promised to giue you a whole pecke of golde.

C. Custance. Perchaunce lacke of a pynte when it shall be all tolde.

M. Mumbl. I would take a gay riche husbande, and I were you.

C. Custance. In good sooth Madge, een so would I, if I were thou.

But no more of this fond talke now, let vs go in,

And see thou no more moue me folly to begin.

Nor bring mee no mo letters for no mans pleasure,

But thou know from whom.

M. Mumbl. I warrant ye shall be sure.

Actus. ij. Scæna. j.

Dobinet Doughtie.

D. Dough.

Here is the house I goe to, before or behinde?

I know not where nor when nor how I shal it finde.

If I had ten mens bodies and legs and strength,

This trotting that I haue must needes lame me at length.

And nowe that my maister is new set on wowyng,

Roister Doister

I trust there shall none of vs finde lacke of doyng:

Two paire of shoes a day will nowe be too litle

To serue me, I must trotte to and fro so mickle.

Go beare me thys token, carrie me this letter,

Nowe this is the best way, nowe that way is better.

Vp before day sirs, I charge you, an houre or twaine,

Trudge, do me thys message, and bring worde quicke againe,

If one misse but a minute, then his armes and woundes,

I woulde not haue slacked for ten thousand poundes.

Nay see I befeeche you, if my most trustie page,

Goe not nowe aboute to hinder my mariage,

So feruent hotte wowyng, and so farre from wiuing,

I trowe neuer was any creature liuyng,

With euery woman is he in some loues pang,

Then vp to our lute at midnight, twangledome twang,

Then twang with our sonets, and twang with our dumps,

And heyhough from our heart, as heauie as lead lumpess:

Then to our recorder with toodleloodle poope

As the howlet out of an yuie bushe should hoope.

Anon to our gitterne, thrumpledum, thrumpledum thrum,

Thrumpledum, thrumpledum, thrumpledum, thrumpledum thrum.

Of Songs and Balades also he is a maker,

And that can he as finely doe as Iacke Raker,

Yea and *extempore* will he dities compose,

33

Foolishe *Marsias* nere made the like I suppose,

Yet must we sing them, as good stuffe I vndertake,

As for such a pen man is well fittyng to make.

Ah for these long nights, heyhow, when will it be day?

I feare ere I come she will be wowed away.

Then when aunswere is made that it may not bee,

O death why commest thou not? by and by (sayth he)

But then, from his heart to put away sorowe,

He is as farre in with some newe loue next morowe.

But in the meane season we trudge and we trot,

From dayspring to midnyght, I sit not, nor rest not.

And now am I sent to dame Christian Custance:

But I feare it will ende with a mocke for pastance.

I bring hir a ring, with a token in a cloute,

And by all gesse, this same is hir house out of doute.

I knowe it nowe perfect, I am in my right way.

And loe yond the olde nourse that was wyth vs last day.

Actus. ij. Scæna. ij.

Mage Mumblecrust. Dobinet Doughtie.

M. Mumbl.

I was nere so shoke vp afore since I was borne,

That our mistresse coulde not haue chid I wold haue sworne:

And I pray God I die if I ment any harme,

But for my life time this shall be to me a charme.

D. Dough. God you saue and see nurse, and howe is it with you?

M. Mumbl. Mary a great deale the worse it is for suche as thou.

D. Dough. For me? Why so?

M. Mumb. Why wer not thou one of them, say,

That song and playde here with the gentleman last day?

D. Dough. Yes, and he would know if you haue for him spoken.

And prayes you to deliuer this ring and token.

M. Mumbl. Nowe by the token that God tokened brother,

I will deliuer no token one nor other.

I haue once ben so shent for your maisters pleasure,

As I will not be agayne for all hys treasure.

D. Dough. He will thank you woman.

M. Mumbl. I will none of his thanke. Ex.

D. Dough. I weene I am a prophete, this geare will proue blanke:

But what should I home againe without answere go?

It were better go to *Rome* on my head than so.

I will tary here this moneth, but some of the house

Shall take it of me, and then I care not a louse.

But yonder commeth forth a wenche or a ladde,

If he haue not one Lumbardes touche, my lucke is bad.

Actus. ij. Scæna. iij.

Truepenie. D. Dough. Tibet T. Anot Al.

Trupeny.

I am cleane lost for lacke of mery companie,

We gree not halfe well within, our wenches and I,

They will commaunde like mistresses, they will forbyd,

If they be not serued, Trupeny must be chyd.

Let them be as mery nowe as ye can desire,

With turnyng of a hande, our mirth lieth in the mire,

I can not skill of such chaungeable mettle,

There is nothing with them but in docke out nettle.

D. Dough. Whether is it better that speake to him furst,

Or he first to me, it is good to cast the wurst.

If I beginne first, he will smell all my purpose,

Otherwise I shall not neede any thing to disclose.

Trupeny. What boy haue we yonder? I will see what he is.

D. Dough. He commeth to me. It is hereabout ywis.

Trupeny. Wouldest thou ought friende, that thou lookest so about?

D. Dough. Yea, but whether ye can helpe me or no, I dout.

35

I seeke to one mistresse Custance house here dwellyng.

Trupenie. It is my mistresse ye seeke too by your telling.

D. Dough. Is there any of that name heere but shee?

Trupenie. Not one in all the whole towne that I knowe pardee.

D. Dough. A Widowe she is I trow.

Trupenie. And what and she be?

D. Dough. But ensured to an husbande.

Trupenie. Yea, so thinke we.

D. Dough. And I dwell with hir husbande that trusteth to be.

Trupenie. In faith then, must thou needes be welcome to me,

Let vs for acquaintance shake handes togither,

And what ere thou be, heartily welcome hither.

Tib. Talk. Well Trupenie neuer but flinging.

An. Alyface. And frisking?

Trupenie. Well Tibet and Annot, still swingyng and whiskyng?

Tib. Talk. But ye roile abroade.

An. Alyface. In the streete euere where.

Trupenie. Where are ye twaine, in chambers when ye mete me there?

But come hither fooles, I haue one nowe by the hande,

Seruant to hym that must be our mistresse husbande,

Byd him welcome.

An. Alyface. To me truly is he welcome.

Tib. Talk. Forsooth and as I may say, heartily welcome.

D. Dough. I thank you mistresse maides

An. Alyface. I hope we shal better know

Tib. Talk. And when wil our new master come.

D. Dough. Shortly I trow.

Tib. Talk. I would it were to morow: for till he resorte

Our mistresse being a Widow hath small comforte,

And I hearde our nourse speake of an husbande to day

Ready for our mistresse, a riche man and a gay,

And we shall go in our frenche hoodes euery day,

In our silke cassocks (I warrant you) freshe and gay,

In our tricke serdegews and billiments of golde,

Braue in our sutes of chaunge seuen double folde,

Then shall ye see Tibet sirs, treade the mosse so trimme,

Nay, why sayd I treade? ye shall see hir glide and swimme,

Not lumperdee clumperdee like our spaniell Rig.

Trupeny. Mary then prickmedaintie come toste me a fig,

Who shall then know our Tib Talke apace trow ye?

An. Alyface. And why not Annot Alyface as fyne as she?

Trupeny. And what had Tom Trupeny, a father or none?

An. Alyface. Then our prety newe come man will looke to be one.

Trupeny. We foure I trust shall be a ioily mery knot.

Shall we sing a fitte to welcome our friende, Annot?

An. Alyface. Perchaunce he can not sing.

D. Dough. I am at all assayes.

Tib. Talk. By cocke and the better welcome to vs alwayes.

Here they sing.

A thing very fitte	No man for despite,
For them that haue witte,	By worde or by write
And are felowes knitte	His felowe to twite,
Seruants in one house to bee,	But further in honestie,
Is fast fast for to sitte,	No good turnes entwite,
And not oft to flitte,	Nor olde sores recite,
Nor varie a whitte,	But let all goe quite,
But louingly to agree.	And louingly to agree.

41

No man complainyng,	After drudgerie,
Nor other disdayning,	When they be werie,
For losse or for gainyng,	Then to be merie,
But felowes or friends to bee.	To laugh and sing they be free
No grudge remainyng,	With chip and cherie
No worke refrainyng,	Heigh derie derie,
Nor helpe restrainyng,	Trill on the berie,
But louingly to agree.	And louingly to agree.
	Finis.

Tib. Talk. Wyll you now in with vs vnto our mistresse go?

D. Dough. I haue first for my maister an errand or two.

But I haue here from him a token and a ring,

They shall haue moste thanke of hir that first doth it bring.

Tib. Talk. Mary that will I.

Trupeny. See and Tibet snatch not now.

Tib. Talk. And why may not I sir, get thanks as well as you? Exeat.

An. Alyface. Yet get ye not all, we will go with you both.

And haue part of your thanks be ye neuer so loth. [Exeant omnes.

D. Dough. So my handes are ridde of it: I care for no more.

I may now return home: so durst I not afore. Exeat.

Actus. ij. Scæna. iiij.

C. Custance. Tibet. Annot Alyface. Trupeny.

C. Custance.

Ay come forth all three: and come hither pretie mayde:

Will not so many forewarnings make you afrayde?

Tib. Talk. Yes forsoth.

C. Custance. But stil be a runner vp and downe

Still be a bringer of tidings and tokens to towne.

Tib. Talk. No forsoth mistresse.

C. Custance. Is all your delite and ioy

In whiskyng and ramping abroade like a Tom boy.

Tib. Talk. Forsoth these were there too, Annot and Trupenie.

Trupenie. Yea but ye alone tooke it, ye can not denie.

Annot Aly. Yea that ye did.

Tibet. But if I had not, ye twaine would.

C. Custance. You great calfe ye should haue more witte, so ye should:

But why shoulde any of you take such things in hande?

Tibet. Because it came from him that must be your husbande.

C. Custance. How do ye know that?

Tibet. Forsoth the boy did say so.

C. Custance. What was his name?

An. Alyface. We asked not.

C. Custance. No did?

An. Aliface. He is not farre gone of likelyhod.

Trupeny. I will see.

C. Custance. If thou canst finde him in the streete bring him to me.

Trupenie. Yes. Exeat.

C. Custance. Well ye naughty girles, if euer I perceiue

That henceforth you do letters or tokens receiue,

To bring vnto me from any person or place,

Except ye first shewe me the partie face to face,

Eyther thou or thou, full truly abye thou shalt.

Tibet. Pardon this, and the next tyme pouder me in falt.

C. Custance. I shall make all girles by you twaine to beware.

Tibet. If euer I offende againe do not me spare.

But if euer I see that false boy any more

By your mistreshyps licence I tell you afore

I will rather haue my cote twentie times swinged,

Than on the naughtie wag not to be auenged.

C. Custance. Good wenches would not so rampe abrode ydelly,

But keepe within doores, and plie their work earnestly,

If one would speake with me that is a man likely,

Ye shall haue right good thanke to bring me worde quickly.

But otherwyse with messages to come in post

From henceforth I promise you, shall be to your cost.

Get you in to your work.

Tib. An. Yes forsoth.

C. Custance. Hence both twaine.

And let me see you play me such a part againe.

Trupeny. Maistresse, I haue runne past the farre ende of the streete,

Yet can I not yonder craftie boy see nor meete.

C. Custance. No?

Trupeny. Yet I looked as farre beyonde the people.

As one may see out of the toppe of Paules steeple.

C. Custance. Hence in at doores, and let me no more be vext.

Trupeny. Forgeue me this one fault, and lay on for the next.

C. Custance. Now will I in too, for I thinke so God

me mende,

This will proue some foolishe matter in the ende. Exeat.

Actus. [i]ij. Scæna. j.

Mathewe Merygreeke.

M. Mery.

Nowe say thys againe: he hath somewhat to dooing

Which followeth the trace of one that is wowing,

Specially that hath no more wit in his hedde,

Than my cousin Roister Doister withall is ledde.

I am sent in all haste to espie and to marke

How our letters and tokens are likely to warke.

Maister Roister Doister must haue aunswere in haste

For he loueth not to spende much labour in waste.

Nowe as for Christian Custance by this light,

Though she had not hir trouth to Gawin Goodluck plight,

Yet rather than with such a loutishe dolte to marie,

I dare say woulde lyue a poore lyfe solitarie,

But fayne would I speake with Custance if I wist how

To laugh at the matter, yond commeth one forth now.

Actus. iij. Scæna. ij.

Tibet. M. Merygreeke. Christian Custance.

Tib. Talk.

AH that I might but once in my life haue a sight

Of him that made vs all so yll shent by this light,

He should neuer escape if I had him by the eare,

But euen from his head, I would it bite or teare.

Yea and if one of them were not inowe,

40

I would bite them both off, I make God auow.

M. Mery. What is he, whome this little mouse doth so threaten?

Tib. Talk. I woulde teache him I trow, to make girles shent or beaten.

M. Mery. I will call hir: Maide with whome are ye so hastie?

Tib. Talk. Not with you sir, but with a little wag-pastie,

A deceiuer of folkes, by subtill craft and guile.

M. Mery. I knowe where she is: Dobinet hath wrought some wile.

Tib. Talk. He brought a ring and token which he sayd was sent

From our dames husbande, but I wot well I was shent:

For it liked hir as well to tell you no lies,

As water in hir shyppe, or salt cast in hir eies:

And yet whence it came neyther we nor she can tell.

M. Mery. We shall haue sport anone: I like this very well.

And dwell ye here with mistresse Custance faire maide?

Tib. Talk. Yea mary doe I sir: what would ye haue sayd?

M. Mery. A little message vnto hir by worde of mouth.

Tib. Talk. No messages by your leaue, nor tokens forsoth.

M. Mery. Then help me to speke with hir.

Tibet. With a good wil that.

Here she commeth forth. Now speake ye know best what.

C. Custance. None other life with you maide, but abrode to skip?

Tib. Talk. Forsoth here is one would speake with your mistresship.

C. Custance. Ah, haue ye ben learning of mo messages now?

Tib. Talk. I would not heare his minde, but bad him shewe it to you.

C. Custance. In at dores.

Tib. Talk. I am gon. Ex.

M. Mery. Dame Custance god ye saue.

C. Custance. Welcome friend Merygreeke: and

what thing wold ye haue?

M. Mery. I am come to you a little matter to breake.

41

C. Custance. But see it be honest, else better not to speake.

M. Mery. Howe feele ye your selfe affected here of late?

C. Custance. I feele no maner chaunge but after the olde rate.

But wherby do ye meane?

M. Mery. Concerning mariage.

Doth not loue lade you?

C. Custance. I feele no such cariage.

M. Mery. Doe ye feele no pangues of dotage?

aunswere me right.

C. Custance. I dote so, that I make but one sleepe all the night

But what neede all these wordes?

M. Mery. Oh Iesus, will ye see

What dissemblyng creatures these same women be?

The gentleman ye wote of, whome ye doe so loue,

That ye woulde fayne marrie him, yf ye durst it moue,

Emong other riche widowes, which are of him glad,

Lest ye for lesing of him perchaunce might runne mad,

Is nowe contented that vpon your sute making,

Ye be as one in election of taking.

C. Custance. What a tale is this? that I wote of?

whome I loue?

M. Mery. Yea and he is as louing a worme againe as a doue.

Een of very pitie he is willyng you to take,

Bicause ye shall not destroy your selfe for his sake.

C. Custance. Mary God yelde his mashyp what euer he be,

It is gentmanly spoken.

M. Mery. Is it not trowe ye?

If ye haue the grace now to offer your self, ye speede.

C. Custance. As muche as though I did, this time it shall not neede,

But what gentman is it, I pray you tell me plaine, That woweth so finely?

M. Mery. Lo where ye be againe,

As though ye knewe him not.

C. Custance. Tush ye speake in iest.

M. Mery. Nay sure, the partie is in good knacking earnest,

42

And haue you he will (he sayth) and haue you he must.

C. Custance. I am promised duryng my life, that is iust.

M. Mery. Mary so thinketh he, vnto him alone.

C. Custance. No creature hath my faith and trouth but one,

That is Gawin Goodlucke: and if it be not hee,

He hath no title this way what euer he be,

Nor I know none to whome I haue such worde spoken.

M. Mery. Ye knowe him not you by his letter and token.

C. Custance. In dede true it is, that a letter I haue,

But I neuer reade it yet as God me saue.

M. Mery. Ye a woman? and your letter so long vnredde.

C. Custance. Ye may therby know what hast I haue to wedde.

But now who it is, for my hande I knowe by gesse.

M. Mery. Ah well I say.

C. Custance. It is Roister Doister doubtlesse.

M. Mery. Will ye neuer leaue this dissimulation?

Ye know hym not.

C. Custance. But by imagination,

For no man there is but a very dolt and loute

That to wowe a Widowe woulde so go about.

He shall neuer haue me hys wife while he doe liue.

M. Mery. Then will he haue you if he may, so mote I thriue,

And he biddeth you sende him worde by me,

That ye humbly beseech him, ye may his wife be,

And that there shall be no let in you nor mistrust,

But to be wedded on sunday next if he lust,

And biddeth you to looke for him.

C. Custance. Doth he byd so?

M. Mery. When he commeth, aske hym whether he did or no?

C. Custance. Goe say, that I bid him keepe him warme at home

For if he come abroade, he shall cough me a mome.

My mynde was vexed, I shrew his head sottish dolt.

M. Mery. He hath in his head.

C. Custance. As much braine as a burbolt.

M. Mery. Well dame Custance, if he heare you thus play choploge.

C. Custance. What will he?

M. Mery. Play the deuill in the horologe.

C. Custance. I defye him loute.

M. Mery. Shall I tell hym what ye say?

C. Custance. Yea and adde what so euer thou canst, I thee pray,

And I will auouche it what so euer it bee.

M. Mery. Then let me alone we will laugh well ye shall see,

It will not be long ere he will hither resorte.

C. Custance. Let hym come when hym lust, I wishe no better sport.

Fare ye well, I will in, and read my great letter.

I shall to my wower make answere the better. Exeat.

Actus. iij. Scæna. iij.

Mathew Merygreeke. Roister Doister.

M. Mery.

Owe that the whole answere in my deuise doth rest,

I shall paint out our wower in colours of the best.

And all that I say shall be on Custances mouth,

She is author of all that I shall speake forsoth.

But yond commeth Roister Doister nowe in a traunce.

R. Royster. Iuno sende me this day good lucke and good chaunce.

I can not but come see how Merygreeke doth speede.

M. Mery. I will not see him, but giue him a iutte in deede.

I crie your mastershyp mercie.

R. Royster. And whither now?

M. Mery. As fast as I could runne sir in poste against you.

But why speake ye so faintly, or why are ye so sad?

R. Royster. Thou knowest the prouerbe, bycause I can not be had.

Hast thou spoken with this woman?

M. Mery. Yea that I haue.

R. Royster. And what will this geare be?

M. Mery. No so God me saue.

R. Royster. Hast thou a flat answer?

M. Mery. Nay a sharp answer.

R. Royster. What

M. Mery. Ye shall not (she sayth) by hir will marry hir cat.

Ye are such a calfe, such an asse, such a blocke,

Such a lilburne, such a hoball, such a lobcocke,

And bicause ye shoulde come to hir at no season,

She despised your maship out of all reason.

Bawawe what ye say (ko I) of such a ientman,

Nay I feare him not (ko she) doe the best he can.

He vaunteth him selfe for a man of prowesse greate,

Where as a good gander I dare say may him beate.

And where he is louted and laughed to skorne,

For the veriest dolte that euer was borne,

And veriest lubber, slouen and beast,

Liuing in this worlde from the west to the east:

Yet of himselfe hath he suche opinion,

That in all the worlde is not the like minion.

He thinketh eche woman to be brought in dotage

With the onely sight of his goodly personage:

Yet none that will haue hym: we do hym loute and flocke,

And make him among vs, our common sporting stocke,

And so would I now (ko she) saue onely bicause,

Better nay (ko I) I lust not medle with dawes.

Ye are happy (ko I) that ye are a woman,

This would cost you your life in case ye were a man.

R. Royster. Yea an hundred thousand pound should not saue hir life.

M. Mery. No but that ye wowe hir to haue hir to your wife,

But I coulde not stoppe hir mouth.

R. Royster. Heigh how alas,

M. Mery. Be of good cheere man, and let the worlde passe.

R. Royster. What shall I doe or say nowe that it will not bee.

45

M. Mery. Ye shall haue choise of a thousande as good as shee,

And ye must pardon hir, it is for lacke of witte.

R. Royster. Yea, for were not I an husbande for hir fitte?

Well what should I now doe?

M. Mery. In faith I can not tell.

R. Royster. I will go home and die.

M. Mery. Then shall I bidde toll the bell?

R. Royster. No.

M. Mery. God haue mercie on your soule, ah good gentleman,

That er ye shuld th[u]s dye for an vnkinde woman.

Will ye drinke once ere ye goe.

R. Royster. No, no, I will none.

M. Mery. How feele your soule to God.

R. Royster. I am nigh gone.

M. Mery. And shall we hence streight?

R. Royster. Yea.

M. Mery. *Placebo dilexi.* vt infra. *

Maister Doister Doister will streight go home and die.

R. Royster. Heigh how, alas, the pangs of death my hearte do breake.

M. Mery. Holde your peace for shame sir, a dead man may not speake.

Nequando: What mourners and what torches shall we haue?

R. Royster. None.

M. Mery. *Dirige.* He will go darklyng to his graue,

Neque, lux, neque crux, neque mourners, *neque* clinke,

He will steale to heauen, vnknowing to God I thinke.

A porta inferi, who shall your goodes possesse?

R. Royster. Thou shalt be my sectour, and haue all more and lesse.

M. Mery. *Requiem æternam.* Now God reward your mastershyp.

And I will crie halfepenie doale for your worshyp. Euocat seruos militis.

Come forth sirs, heare the dolefull newes I shall you tell.

Our good maister here will no longer with vs dwell,

46

But in spite of Custance, which hath hym weried,

Let vs see his mashyp solemnely buried.

And while some piece of his soule is yet hym within,

Some part of his funeralls let vs here begin.

Audiui vocem, All men take heede by this one gentleman,

Howe you sette your loue vpon an vnkinde woman.

For these women be all such madde pieuishe elues,

They will not be wonne except it please them selues.

But in fayth Custance if euer ye come in hell,

Maister Roister Doister shall serue you as well.

And will ye needes go from vs thus in very deede?

R. Royster. Yea in good sadnesse?

M. Mery. Now Iesus Christ be your speede.

Good night Roger olde knaue, farewell Roger olde knaue,

Good night Roger olde knaue, knaue knap. vt infra. **

Pray for the late maister Roister Doisters soule,

And come forth parish Clarke, let the passing bell toll.

Pray for your mayster sirs, and for hym ring a peale. Ad seruos militis.

He was your right good maister while he was in heale.

Qui Lazarum.

R. Royster. Heigh how.

M. Mery. Dead men go not so fast In Paradisum.

R. Royster. Heihow.

M. Mery. Soft, heare what I haue cast

R. Royster. I will heare nothing, I am past.

M. Mery. Whough, wellaway.

Ye may tarie one houre, and heare what I shall say,

Ye were best sir for a while to reuiue againe,

And quite them er ye go.

R. Royster. Trowest thou so?

M. Mery. Ye plain.

R. Royster. How may I reuiue being nowe so farre past?

M. Mery. I will rubbe your temples, and fette you againe at last.

R. Royster. It will not be possible.

47

M. Mery. Yes for twentie pounde.

R. Royster. Armes what dost thou?

M. Mery. Fet you again out of your sound

By this crosse ye were nigh gone in deede, I might feele

Your soule departing within an inche of your heele.

Now folow my counsell.

R. Royster. What is it?

M. Mery. If I wer you,

Custance should eft seeke to me, ere I woulde bowe.

R. Royster. Well, as thou wilt haue me, euen so will I doe.

M. Mery. Then shall ye reuiue againe for an houre or two.

R. Royster. As thou wilt I am content for a little space.

M. Mery. Good happe is not hastie: yet in space com[e]th grace,

To speake with Custance your selfe shoulde be very well,

What good therof may come, nor I, nor you can tell.

But now the matter standeth vpon your mariage,

Ye must now take vnto you a lustie courage.

Ye may not speake with a faint heart to Custance,

But with a lusty breast and countenance,

That she may knowe she hath to answere to a man.

R. Royster. Yes I can do that as well as any can.

M. Mery. Then bicause ye must Custance face to face wowe,

Let vs see how to behaue your selfe ye can doe.

Ye must haue a portely bragge after your estate.

R. Royster. Tushe, I can handle that after the best rate.

M. Mery. Well done, so loe, vp man with your head and chin,

Vp with that snoute man: so loe, nowe ye begin,

So, that is somewhat like, but prankie cote, nay whan,

That is a lustie brute, handes vnder your side man:

So loe, now is it euen as it should bee,

That is somewhat like, for a man of your degree.

Then must ye stately goe, ietting vp and downe,

Tut, can ye no better shake the taile of your gowne?

There loe, suche a lustie bragge it is ye must make.

R. Royster. To come behind, and make curtsie, thou must som pains take.

M. Mery. Else were I much to blame, I thanke your mastershyp.

The lorde one day all to begrime you with worshyp,

Backe sir sauce, let gentlefolkes haue elbowe roome,

Voyde sirs, see ye not maister Roister Doister come?

Make place my maisters.

R. Royster. Thou iustlest nowe to nigh.

M. Mery. Back al rude loutes.

R. Royster. Tush.

M. Mery. I crie your maship mercy

Hoighdagh, if faire fine mistresse Custance sawe you now,

Ralph Royster Doister were hir owne I warrant you.

R. Royster. Neare an M by your girdle?

M. Mery. Your good mastershyps

Maistershyp, were hir owne Mistreshyps mistreshyps,

Ye were take vp for haukes, ye were gone, ye were gone,

But now one other thing more yet I thinke vpon.

R. Royster. Shewe what it is.

M. Mery. A wower be he neuer so poore

Must play and sing before his bestbeloues doore,

How much more than you?

R. Royster. Thou speakest wel out of dout.

M. Mery. And perchaunce that woulde make hir the sooner come out.

R. Royster. Goe call my Musitians, bydde them high apace.

M. Mery. I wyll be here with them ere ye can say trey ace. Exeat.

R. Royster. This was well sayde of Merygreeke, I lowe hys wit,

Before my sweete hearts dore we will haue a fit,

That if my loue come forth, that I may with hir talke,

I doubt not but this geare shall on my side walke.

But lo, how well Merygreeke is returned sence.

M. Mery. There hath grown no grasse on my heele since I went hence,

49

Lo here haue I brought that shall make you pastance.

R. Royster. Come sirs let vs sing to winne my deare loue Custance.

Cantent.

M. Mery. Lo where she commeth, some countenaunce to hir make

And ye shall heare me be plaine with hir for your sake.

*_ See pp. 87, 88._

**_ See p. 88._

Actus. iij. Scæna. iiij.

Custance. Merygreeke. Roister Doister.

C. Custance.

Hat gaudyng and foolyng is this afore my doore?

M. Mery. May not folks be honest, pray you, though they be pore?

C. Custance. As that thing may be true, so rich folks may be fooles,

R. Royster. Hir talke is as fine as she had learned in schooles.

M. Mery. Looke partly towarde hir, and drawe a little nere.

C. Custance. Get ye home idle folkes.

M. Mery. Why may not we be here?

Nay and ye will haze, haze: otherwise I tell you plaine,

And ye will not haze, then giue vs our geare againe.

C. Custance. In deede I haue of yours much gay things God saue all.

R. Royster. Speake gently vnto hir, and let hir take all.

M. Mery. Ye are to tender hearted: shall she make vs dawes?

Nay dame, I will be plaine with you in my friends cause.

R. Royster. Let all this passe sweete heart and accept my seruice.

50

C. Custance. I will not be serued with a foole in no wise,

When I choose an husbande I hope to take a man.

M. Mery. And where will ye finde one which can doe that he can?

Now thys man towarde you being so kinde,

You not to make him an answere somewhat to his minde.

C. Custance. I sent him a full answere by you dyd I not?

M. Mery. And I reported it.

C. Custance. Nay I must speake it againe.

R. Royster. No no, he tolde it all.

M. Mery. Was I not metely plaine?

R. Royster. Yes.

M. Mery. But I would not tell all, for faith if I had

With you dame Custance ere this houre it had been bad,

And not without cause: for this goodly personage,

Ment no lesse than to ioyne with you in mariage.

C. Custance. Let him wast no more labour nor sute about me.

M. Mery. Ye know not where your preferment lieth I see,

He sending you such a token, ring and letter.

C. Custance. Mary here it is, ye neuer sawe a better.

M. Mery. Let vs see your letter.

C. Custance. Holde, reade it if ye can.

And see what letter it is to winne a woman.

M. Mery. To mine owne deare coney birde, swete heart, and pigsny

Good Mistresse Custance present these by and by,

Of this superscription do ye blame the stile?

C. Custance. With the rest as good stuffe as ye redde a great while.

M. Mery. Sweete mistresse where as I loue you nothing at all,

Regarding your substance and richesse chiefe of all,

For your personage, beautie, demeanour and wit,

I commende me vnto you neuer a whit.

Sorie to heare report of your good welfare.

For (as I heare say) suche your conditions are,

That ye be worthie fauour of no liuing man,

To be abhorred of euery honest man.

To be taken for a woman enclined to vice.

Nothing at all to Vertue gyuing hir due price.

Whersore concerning mariage, ye are thought

Suche a fine Paragon, as nere honest man bought.

And nowe by these presentes I do you aduertise

That I am minded to marrie you in no wise.

For your goodes and substance, I coulde bee content

To take you as ye are. If ye mynde to bee my wyfe,

Ye shall be assured for the tyme of my lyfe,

I will keepe ye ryght well, from good rayment and fare,

Ye shall not be kepte but in sorowe and care.

Ye shall in no wyse lyue at your owne libertie,

Doe and say what ye lust, ye shall neuer please me,

But when ye are mery, I will be all sadde,

When ye are sory, I will be very gladde.

When ye seeke your heartes ease, I will be vnkinde,

At no tyme, in me shall ye muche gentlenesse finde.

But all things contrary to your will and minde,

Shall be done: otherwise I wyll not be behinde

To speake. And as for all them that woulde do you wrong

I will so helpe and mainteyne, ye shall not lyue long.

Nor any foolishe dolte, shall cumbre you but I.

Thus good mistresse Custance, the lorde you saue and kepe,

From me Roister Doister, whether I wake or slepe.

Who fauoureth you no lesse, (ye may be bolde)

Than this letter purporteth, which ye haue vnfolde.

C. Custance. Howe by this letter of loue? is it not fine?

R. Royster. By the armes of Caleys it is none of myne.

M. Mery. Fie you are fowle to blame this is your owne hand.

C. Custance. Might not a woman be proude of such an husbande?

M. Mery. Ah that ye would in a letter shew such despite.

R. Royster. Oh I would I had hym here, the which did it endite.

M. Mery. Why ye made it your selfe ye tolde me by this light.

R. Royster. Yea I ment I wrote it myne owne selfe yesternight.

C. Custance. Ywis sir, I would not haue sent you such a mocke.

R. Royster. Ye may so take it, but I ment it not so by cocke.

M. Mery. Who can blame this woman to fume and frette and rage?

Tut, tut, your selfe nowe haue marde your owne marriage.

Well, yet mistresse Custance, if ye can this remitte,

This gentleman other wise may your loue requitte.

C. Custance. No God be with you both, and seeke no more to me. Exeat.

R. Royster. Wough, she is gone for euer, I shall hir no more see.

M. Mery. What weepe? fye for shame, and blubber? for manhods sake,

Neuer lette your foe so muche pleasure of you take.

Rather play the mans parte, and doe loue refraine.

If she despise you een despise ye hir againe.

R. Royster. By gosse and for thy sake I defye hir in deede.

M. Mery. Yea and perchaunce that way ye shall much sooner speede,

For one madde propretie these women haue in fey,

When ye will, they will not: Will not ye, then will they.

Ah foolishe woman, ah moste vnluckie Custance,

Ah vnfortunate woman, ah pieuishe Custance,

Art thou to thine harmes so obstinately bent,

That thou canst not see where lieth thine high preferment?

Canst thou not lub dis man, which coulde lub dee so well?

Art thou so much thine own foe.

R. Royster. Thou dost the truth tell.

M. Mery. Wel I lament.

R. Royster. So do I.

M. Mery. Wherfor?

53

R. Royster. For this thing

Bicause she is gone.

M. Mery. I mourne for an other thing.

R. Royster. What is it Merygreeke, wherfore thou dost griefe take?

M. Mery. That I am not a woman myselfe for your sake,

I would haue you my selfe, and a strawe for yond Gill,

And mocke much of you though it were against my will.

I would not I warrant you, fall in such a rage,

As so to refuse suche a goodly personage.

R. Royster. In faith I heartily thanke thee Merygreeke.

M. Mery. And I were a woman.

R. Royster. Thou wouldest to me seeke.

M. Mery. For though I say it, a goodly person ye bee.

R. Royster. No, no.

M. Mery. Yes a goodly man as ere I dyd see.

R. Royster. No, I am a poore homely man as God made mee.

M. Mery. By the faith that I owe to God sir, but ye bee.

Woulde I might for your sake, spende a thousande pound land.

R. Royster. I dare say thou wouldest haue me to thy husbande.

M. Mery. Yea: And I were the fairest lady in the shiere,

And knewe you as I know you, and see you nowe here.

Well I say no more.

R. Royster. Gramercies with all my hart.

M. Mery. But since that can not be, will ye play a wise parte?

R. Royster. How should I?

M. Mery. Refraine from Custance a while now.

And I warrant hir soone right glad to seeke to you,

Ye shall see hir anon come on hir knees creeping,

And pray you to be good to hir salte teares weeping.

R. Royster. But what and she come not?

M. Mery. In faith then farewel she.

Or else if ye be wroth, ye may auenged be.

54

R. Royster. By cocks precious potsticke, and een so I shall.

I wyll vtterly destroy hir, and house and all,

But I woulde be auenged in the meane space,

On that vile scribler, that did my wowyng disgrace.

M. Mery. Scribler (ko you) in deede he is worthy no lesse.

I will call hym to you, and ye bidde me doubtlesse.

R. Royster. Yes, for although he had as many liues,

As a thousande widowes, and a thousande wiues,

As a thousande lyons, and a thousand rattes,

A thousande wolues, and a thousande cattes,

A thousande bulles, and a thousande calues,

And a thousande legions diuided in halues,

He shall neuer scape death on my swordes point,

Though I shoulde be torne therfore ioynt by ioynt.

M. Mery. Nay, if ye will kyll him, I will not fette him,

I will not in so muche extremitie sette him,

He may yet amende sir, and be an honest man,

Therfore pardon him good soule, as muche as ye can.

R. Royster. Well, for thy sake, this once with his lyfe he shall passe,

But I wyll hewe hym all to pieces by the Masse.

M. Mery. Nay fayth ye shall promise that he shall no harme haue,

Else I will not fet him.

R. Royster. I shall so God me saue.

But I may chide him a good.

M. Mery. Yea that do hardely.

R. Royster. Go then.

M. Mery. I returne, and bring him to you by and by. Ex.

55

Actus. iij. Scæna. v.

Roister Doister. Mathewe Merygreeke. Scriuener.

R. Royster.

Hat is a gentleman but his worde and his promise?

I must nowe saue this vilaines lyfe in any wise,

And yet at hym already my handes doe tickle,

I shall vneth holde them, they wyll be so fickle.

But lo and Merygreeke haue not brought him sens?

M. Mery. Nay I woulde I had of my purse payde fortie pens.

Scriuener. So woulde I too: but it needed not that stounde,

M. Mery. But the ientman had rather spent fiue thousande pounde,

For it disgraced him at least fiue tymes so muche.

Scriuener. He disgraced hym selfe, his loutishnesse is suche.

R. Royster. Howe long they stande prating? Why comst thou not away?

M. Mery. Come nowe to hymselfe, and hearke what he will say.

Scriuener. I am not afrayde in his presence to appeere.

R. Royster. Arte thou come felow?

Scriuener. How thinke you? am I not here?

R. Royster. What hindrance hast thou done me, and what villanie?

Scriuener. It hath come of thy selfe, if thou hast had any.

R. Royster. All the stocke thou comest of later or rather,

From thy fyrst fathers grandfathers fathers father,

Nor all that shall come of thee to the worldes ende,

Though to three score generations they descende,

Can be able to make me a iust recompense,

For this trespasse of thine and this one offense.

Scriuener. Wherin?

R. Royster. Did not you make me a letter brother?

Scriuener. Pay the like hire, I will make you suche an other.

R. Royster. Nay see and these whooreson Phariseys and Scribes

Doe not get their liuyng by polling and bribes.

If it were not for shame.

Scriuener. Nay holde thy hands still.

M. Mery. Why did ye not promise that ye would not him spill?

Scriuener. Let him not spare me.

R. Royster. Why wilt thou strike me again?

Scriuener. Ye shall haue as good as ye bring of me that is plaine.

M. Mery. I can not blame him sir, though your blowes wold him greue.

For he knoweth present death to ensue of all ye geue.

R. Royster. Well, this man for once hath purchased thy pardon.

Scriuener. And what say ye to me? or else I will be gon.

R. Royster. I say the letter thou madest me was not good.

Scriuener. Then did ye wrong copy it of likelyhood.

R. Royster. Yes, out of thy copy worde for worde I wrote.

Scriuener. Then was it as ye prayed to haue it I wote,

But in reading and pointyng there was made some faulte.

R. Royster. I wote not, but it made all my matter to haulte.

Scriuener. Howe say you, is this mine originall or no?

R. Royster. The selfe same that I wrote out of, so mote I go.

Scriuener. Loke you on your owne fist, and I will looke on this,

And let this man be iudge whether I reade amisse.

To myne owne dere coney birde, sweete heart, and

57

Good mistresse Custance, present these by and by.

How now? doth not this superscription agree?

R. Royster. Reade that is within, and there ye shall the fault see.

Scriuener. Sweete mistresse, where as I loue you, nothing at all

Regarding your richesse and substance: chiefe of all

For your personage, beautie, demeanour and witte

I commende me vnto you: Neuer a whitte

Sory to heare reporte of your good welfare.

For (as I heare say) suche your conditions are,

That ye be worthie fauour: Of no liuing man

To be abhorred: of euery honest man

To be taken for a woman enclined to vice

Nothing at all: to vertue giuing hir due price.

Wherfore concerning mariage, ye are thought

Suche a fine Paragon, as nere honest man bought.

And nowe by these presents I doe you aduertise,

That I am minded to marrie you: In no wyse

For your goodes and substance: I can be content

To take you as you are: yf ye will be my wife,

Ye shall be assured for the time of my life,

I wyll keepe you right well: from good raiment and fare,

Ye shall not be kept: but in sorowe and care

Ye shall in no wyse lyue: at your owne libertie,

Doe and say what ye lust: ye shall neuer please me

But when ye are merrie: I will bee all sadde

When ye are sorie: I wyll be very gladde

When ye seeke your heartes ease: I will be vnkinde

At no time: in me shall ye muche gentlenesse finde.

But all things contrary to your will and minde

Shall be done otherwise: I wyll not be behynde

To speake: And as for all they that woulde do you wrong,

(I wyll so helpe and maintayne ye) shall not lyue long.

Nor any foolishe dolte shall cumber you, but I,

I, who ere say nay, wyll sticke by you tyll I die.

Thus good mistresse Custance, the lorde you saue and kepe.

From me Roister Doister, whether I wake or slepe,

58

Who fauoureth you no lesse, (ye may be bolde)

Than this letter purporteth, which ye haue vnfolde.

Now sir, what default can ye finde in this letter?

R. Royster. Of truth in my mynde there can not be a better.

Scriuener. Then was the fault in readyng, and not in writyng,

No nor I dare say in the fourme of endityng,

But who read this letter, that it sounded so nought?

M. Mery. I redde it in deede.

Scriuener. Ye red it not as ye ought.

R. Royster. Why thou wretched villaine was all this same fault in thee?

M. Mery. I knocke your costarde if ye offer to strike me.

R. Royster. Strikest thou in deede? and I offer but in iest?

M. Mery. Yea and rappe you againe except ye can sit in rest.

And I will no longer tarie here me beleue.

R. Royster. What wilt thou be angry, and I do thee forgeue?

Fare thou well scribler, I crie thee mercie in deede.

Scriuener. Fare ye well bibbler, and worthily may ye speede.

R. Royster. If it were an other but thou, it were a knaue.

M. Mery. Ye are an other your selfe sir, the lorde vs both saue,

Albeit in this matter I must your pardon craue,

Alas woulde ye wyshe in me the witte that ye haue?

But as for my fault I can quickely amende,

I will shewe Custance it was I that did offende.

R. Royster. By so doing hir anger may be reformed.

M. Mery. But if by no entreatie she will be turned,

Then sette lyght by hir and bee as testie as shee,

And doe your force vpon hir with extremitie.

R. Royster. Come on therefore lette vs go home in sadnesse.

M. Mery. That if force shall neede all may be in a readinesse,

And as for thys letter hardely let all go,

We wyll know where she refuse you for that or no. [Exeant am.

Actus. iiij. Scæna. j.

Sym Suresby.

Sim Sure.

S there any man but I Sym Suresby alone,

That would haue taken such an enterprise him vpon,

In suche an outragious tempest as as this was.

Suche a daungerous gulfe of the sea to passe.

I thinke verily *Neptunes* mightie godshyp,

Was angry with some that was in our shyp,

And but for the honestie which in me he founde,

I thinke for the others sake we had bene drownde.

But fye on that seruant which for his maisters wealth

Will sticke for to hazarde both his lyfe and his health.

My maister Gawyn Goodlucke after me a day

Bicause of the weather, thought best hys shyppe to stay,

And now that I haue the rough sourges so well past,

God graunt I may finde all things safe here at last.

Then will I thinke all my trauaile well spent.

Nowe the first poynt wherfore my maister hath me sent

Is to salute dame Christian Custance his wife,

Espoused: whome he tendreth no lesse than his life,

I must see how it is with hir well or wrong,

And whether for him she doth not now thinke long:

Then to other friendes I haue a message or tway,

And then so to returne and mete him on the way.

Now wyll I goe knocke that I may dispatche with speede,

But loe forth commeth hir selfe happily in deede.

60

Actus. iiij. Scæna. ij.

Christian Custance. Sim. Suresby.

C. Custance.

I come to see if any more stirryng be here,

But what straunger is this, which doth to me appere?

Sym Surs. I will speake to hir: Dame the lorde you saue and see.

C. Custance. What friende Sym Suresby? Forsoth right welcome ye be,

Howe doth mine owne Gawyn Goodlucke, I pray the tell?

S. Suresby. When he knoweth of your health he will be perfect well.

C. Custance. If he haue perfect helth, I am as I would be.

Sim. Sure. Suche newes will please him well, this is as it should be.

C. Custance. I thinke now long for him.

Sym Sure. And he as long for you.

C. Custance. When wil he be at home?

Sym Sure. His heart is here een now

His body commeth after.

C. Custance. I woulde see that faine.

Sim Sure. As fast as wynde and sayle can cary it a maine.

But what two men are yonde comming hitherwarde?

C. Custance. Now I shrew their best Christmasse chekes both togetherward.

Actus. iiij. Scæna. iij.

Christian Custance. Sym Suresby. Ralph Roister. Mathew Merygreke. Trupeny.

C. Custance.

What meane these lewde felowes thus to trouble me stil?

Sym Suresby here perchance shal therof deme som yll,

61

And shall suspect in me some point of naughtinesse,

And they come hitherward.

Sym Sure. What is their businesse?

C. Custance. I haue nought to them, nor they to me in sadnesse.

Sim Sure. Let vs hearken them, somewhat there is I feare it.

R. Royster. I will speake out aloude best, that she may heare it.

M. Mery. Nay alas, ye may so feare hir out of hir wit.

R. Royster. By the crosse of my sworde, I will hurt hir no whit.

M. Mery. Will ye doe no harme in deede, shall I trust your worde?

R. Royster. By Roister Doisters fayth I will speake but in borde.

Sim Sure. Let vs hearken them, somwhat there is I feare it.

R. Royster. I will speake out aloude, I care not who heare it:

Sirs, see that my harnesse, my tergat, and my shield,

Be made as bright now, as when I was last in fielde,

As white as I shoulde to warre againe to morrowe:

For sicke shall I be, but I worke some folke sorow.

Therfore see that all shine as bright as sainct George,

Or as doth a key newly come from the Smiths forge.

I woulde haue my sworde and harnesse to shine so bright,

That I might therwith dimme mine enimies sight,

I would haue it cast beames as fast I tell you playne,

As doth the glittryng grasse after a showre of raine.

And see that in case I shoulde neede to come to arming,

All things may be ready at a minutes warning,

For such chaunce may chaunce in an houre, do ye heare?

M. Mery. As perchance shall not chaunce againe in seuen yeare.

R. Royster. Now draw we neare to hir, and here what shall be sayde.

M. Mery. But I woulde not haue you make hir too muche afrayde.

R. Royster. Well founde sweete wife (I trust) for al this your soure looke.

C. Custance. Wife, why cal ye me wife?

Sim Sure. Wife? this gear goth acrook.

M. Mery. Nay mistresse Custance, I warrant you, our letter

Is not as we redde een nowe, but much better,

And where ye halfe stomaked this gentleman afore,

For this same letter, ye wyll loue hym now therefore,

Nor it is not this letter, though ye were a queene,

That shoulde breake marriage betweene you twaine I weene.

C. Custance. I did not refuse hym for the letters sake.

R. Royster. Then ye are content me for your husbande to take.

C. Custance. You for my husbande to take? nothing lesse truely.

R. Royster. Yea say so, sweete spouse, afore straungers hardly.

M. Mery. And though I haue here his letter of loue with me,

Yet his ryng and tokens he sent, keepe safe with ye.

C. Custance. A mischiefe take his tokens, and him and thee too.

But what prate I with fooles? haue I nought else to doo?

Come in with me Sym Suresby to take some repast.

Sim Sure. I must ere I drinke by your leaue, goe in all hast,

To a place or two, with earnest letters of his.

C. Custance. Then come drink here with me.

Sim Sure. I thank you.

C. Custance. Do not misse

You shall haue a token to your maister with you.

Sym Sure. No tokens this time gramercies, God be with you. Exeat.

C. Custance. Surely this fellowe misdeemeth some yll in me.

Which thing but God helpe, will go neere to spill me.

R. Royster. Yea farewell fellow, and tell thy maister Goodlucke

That he commeth to late of thys blossome to plucke.

Let him keepe him there still, or at least wise make no hast,

As for his labour hither he shall spende in wast.

63

His betters be in place nowe.

M. Mery. As long as it will hold.

C. Custance. I will be euen with thee thou beast, thou mayst be bolde.

R. Royster. Will ye haue vs then?

C. Custance. I will neuer haue thee.

R. Royster. Then will I haue you?

C. Custance. No, the deuill shal haue thee.

I haue gotten this houre more shame and harme by thee,

Then all thy life days thou canst do me honestie.

M. Mery. Why nowe may ye see what it comth too in the ende,

To make a deadly foe of your most louing frende:

And ywis this letter if ye woulde heare it now.

C. Custance. I will heare none of it.

M. Mery. In faith would rauishe you.

C. Custance. He hath stained my name for euer this is cleare.

R. Royster. I can make all as well in an houre.

M. Mery. As ten yeare.

How say ye, wil ye haue him?

C. Custance. No.

M. Mery. Wil ye take him?

C. Custance. I defie him.

M. Mery. At my word?

C. Custance. A shame take him.

Waste no more wynde, for it will neuer bee.

M. Mery. This one faulte with twaine shall be mended, ye shall see.

Gentle mistresse Custance now, good mistresse Custance,

Honey mistresse Custance now, sweete mistresse Custance,

Golden mistresse Custance now, white mistresse Custance,

Silken mistresse Custance now, faire mistresse Custance.

C. Custance. Faith rather than to mary with suche a doltishe loute,

I woulde matche my selfe with a begger out of doute.

M. Mery. Then I can say no more, to speede we are not like,

Except ye rappe out a ragge of your Rhetorike.

C. Custance. Speake not of winnyng me: for it shall neuer be so.

64

R. Royster. Yes dame, I will haue you whether ye will or no,

I commaunde you to loue me, wherfore shoulde ye not?

Is not my loue to you chafing and burning hot?

M. Mery. Too hir, that is well sayd.

R. Royster. Shall I so breake my braine

To dote vpon you, and ye not loue vs againe?

M. Mery. Wel sayd yet.

C. Custance. Go to you goose.

R. Royster. I say Kit Custance,

In case ye will not haze, well, better yes perchaunce.

C. Custance. Auaunt lozell, picke thee hence.

M. Mery. Wel sir, ye perceiue,

For all your kinde offer, she will not you receiue.

R. Royster. Then a strawe for hir, and a strawe for hir againe,

She shall not be my wife, woulde she neuer so faine,

No and though she would be at ten thousand pounde cost.

M. Mery. Lo dame, ye may see what an husbande ye haue lost.

C. Custance. Yea, no force, a iewell muche better lost than founde.

M. Mery. Ah, ye will not beleue how this doth my heart wounde.

How shoulde a mariage betwene you be towarde,

If both parties drawe backe, and become so frowarde.

R. Royster. Nay dame, I will fire thee out of thy house,

And destroy thee and all thine, and that by and by.

M. Mery. Nay for the passion of God sir, do not so.

R. Royster. Yes, except she will say yea to that she sayde no.

C. Custance. And what, be there no officers trow we, in towne

To checke idle loytrers, braggyng vp and downe?

Where be they, by whome vacabunds shoulde be represt?

That poore sillie Widowes might liue in peace and rest.

Shall I neuer ridde thee out of my companie?

I will call for helpe, what hough, come forth Trupenie.

Trupenie. Anon. What is your will mistresse? dyd ye call me?

C. Custance. Yea, go runne apace, and as fast as may be,

Pray Tristram Trusty, my moste assured frende,

To be here by and by, that he may me defende.

Trupenie. That message so quickly shall be done by Gods grace,

That at my returne ye shall say, I went apace. Exeat.

C. Custance. Then shall we see I trowe, whether ye shall do me harme,

R. Royster. Yes in faith Kitte, I shall thee and thine so charme,

That all women incarnate by thee may beware.

C. Custance. Nay, as for charming me, come hither if thou dare,

I shall cloute thee tyll thou stinke, both thee and thy traine,

And coyle thee mine owne handes, and sende thee home againe.

R. Royster. Yea sayst thou me that dame? dost thou me threaten?

Goe we, I still see whether I shall be beaten.

M. Mery. Nay for the paishe of God, let me now treate peace,

For bloudshed will there be in case this strife increace.

Ah good dame Custance, take better way with you.

R. Royster. Let him do his worst.

M. Mery. Yeld in time.

R. Royster. Come hence thou.

Exeant Roister et Mery.

Actus. iiij. Scæna. iiij.

Christian Custance. Anot Alyface. Tibet T. M. Mumblecrust.

C. Custance.

O sirra, if I should not with hym take this way,

I should not be ridde of him I thinke till doomes day,

66

I will call forth my folkes, that without any mockes

If he come agayne we may giue him rappes and knockes.

Mage Mumblecrust, come forth, and Tibet Talke apace.

Yea and come forth too, mistresse Annot Alyface.

Annot Aly. I come.

Tibet. And I am here.

M. Mumb. And I am here too at length.

C. Custance. Like warriers if nede bee, ye must shew your strength

The man that this day hath thus begiled you,

Is Ralph Roister Doister, whome ye know well mowe,

The moste loute and dastarde that euer on grounde trode.

Tib. Talk. I see all folke mocke hym when he goth abrode.

C. Custance. What pretie maide? will ye talke when I speake?

Tib. Talk. No forsooth good mistresse.

C. Custance. Will ye my tale breake?

He threatneth to come hither with all his force to fight,

I charge you if he come, on him with all your might.

M. Mumbl. I with my distaffe will reache hym one rappe,

Tib. Talk. And I with my newe broome will sweepe hym one swappe,

And then with our greate clubbe I will reache hym one rappe.

An. Aliface. And I with our skimmer will fling him one flappe.

Tib. Talk. Then Trupenies firesorke will him shrewdly fray,

And you with the spitte may driue him quite away.

C. Custance. Go make all ready, that it may be een so.

Tib. Talk. For my parte I shrewe them that last about it go. Exeant.

67

Actus. iiij. Scæna. v.

Christian Custance. Trupenie. Tristram Trusty.

C. Custance.

Rupenie dyd promise me to runne a great pace,

My friend Tristram Trusty to fet into this place.

In deede he dwelleth hence a good stert I confesse:

But yet a quicke messanger might twice since as I gesse,

Haue gone and come againe. Ah yond I spie him now.

Trupeny. Ye are a slow goer sir, I make God auow.

My mistresse Custance will in me put all the blame,

Your leggs be longer than myne: come apace for shame.

C. Custance. I can thee thanke Trupenie, thou hast done right wele.

Trupeny. Maistresse since I went no grasse hath growne on my hele,

But maister Tristram Trustie here maketh no speede.

C. Custance. That he came at all I thanke him in very deede,

For now haue I neede of the helpe of some wise man.

T. Trusty. Then may I be gone againe, for none such I [a]m.

Trupenie. Ye may bee by your going: for no Alderman

Can goe I dare say, a sadder pace than ye can.

C. Custance. Trupenie get thee in, thou shalt among them knowe,

How to vse thy selfe, like a propre man I trowe.

Trupeny. I go. Ex.

C. Custance. Now Tristram Trusty I thank you right much.

For at my first sending to come ye neuer grutch.

T. Trusty. Dame Custance God ye saue, and while my life shall last,

For my friende Goodlucks sake ye shall not sende in wast.

C. Custance. He shal giue you thanks.

T. Trusty. I will do much for his sake

C. Custance. But alack, I feare, great displeasure shall be take.

T. Trusty. Wherfore?

C. Custance. For a foolish matter.

T. Trusty. What is your cause

C. Custance. I am yll accombred with a couple of dawes.

T. Trusty. Nay weepe not woman: but tell me what your cause is

As concerning my friende is any thing amisse?

C. Custance. No not on my part: but here was Sym Suresby.

T. Trustie. He was with me and told me so.

C. Custance. And he stoode by

While Ralph Roister Doister with helpe of Merygreeke,

For promise of mariage dyd vnto me seeke.

T. Trusty. And had ye made any promise before them twaine,

C. Custance. No I had rather be torne in pieces and slaine,

No man hath my faith and trouth, but Gawyn Goodlucke,

And that before Suresby dyd I say, and there stucke,

But of certaine letters there were suche words spoken.

T. Trustie. He tolde me that too.

C. Custance. And of a ring and token.

That Suresby I spied, dyd more than halfe suspect,

That I my faith to Gawyn Goodlucke dyd reiect.

T. Trusty. But there was no such matter dame Custance in deede?

C. Custance. If euer my head thought it, God sende me yll speede.

Wherfore I beseech you, with me to be a witnesse,

That in all my lyfe I neuer intended thing lesse,

And what a brainsicke foole Ralph Roister Doister is,

Your selfe know well enough.

T. Trusty. Ye say full true ywis.

C. Custance. Bicause to bee his wife I ne graunt nor apply,

Hither will he com he sweareth by and by,

To kill both me and myne, and beate downe my house flat.

Therfore I pray your aide.

T. Trustie. I warrant you that.

C. Custance. Haue I so many yeres liued a sobre life,

And shewed my selfe honest, mayde, widowe, and wyfe

And nowe to be abused in such a vile sorte,

Ye see howe poore Widowes lyue all voyde of comfort.

T. Trusty. I warrant hym do you no harme nor wrong at all.

C. Custance. No, but Mathew Merygreeke doth me most appall,

That he woulde ioyne hym selfe with suche a wretched loute.

T. Trusty. He doth it for a iest I knowe hym out of doubte,

And here cometh Merygreke.

C. Custance. Then shal we here his mind.

Actus. iiij. Scæna. vj.

Merygreke. Christian Custance. Trist. Trusty.

M. Mery.

Ustance and Trustie both, I doe you here well finde.

C. Custance. Ah Mathew Merygreeke, ye haue vsed me well.

M. Mery. Nowe for altogether ye must your answere tell.

Will ye haue this man, woman? or else will ye not?

Else will he come neuer bore so brymme nor tost so hot.

Tris. and Cu. But why ioyn ye with him.

T. Trusty. For mirth.

C. Custance. Or else in sadnesse

M. Mery. The more fond of you both hardly yat mater gesse.

Tristram. Lo how say ye dame?

M. Mery. Why do ye thinke dame Custance

That in this wowyng I haue ment ought but pastance?

C. Custance. Much things ye spake, I wote, to maintaine his dotage.

M. Mery. But well might ye iudge I spake it all in mockage?

For why? Is Roister Doister a fitte husband for you?

70

T. Trusty. I dare say ye neuer thought it.

M. Mery. No to God I vow.

And dyd not I knowe afore of the insurance

Betweene Gawyn Goodlucke, and Christian Custance?

And dyd not I for the nonce, by my conueyance,

Reade his letter in a wrong sense for daliance?

That if you coulde haue take it vp at the first bounde,

We should therat such a sporte and pastime haue founde,

That all the whole towne should haue ben the merier.

C. Custance. Ill ake your heades both, I was neuer werier,

Nor neuer more vexte since the first day I was borne.

T. Trusty. But very well I wist he here did all in scorne.

C. Custance. But I feared therof to take dishonestie.

M. Mery. This should both haue made sport, and shewed your honestie

And Goodlucke I dare sweare, your witte therin would low.

T. Trusty. Yea, being no worse than we know it to be now.

M. Mery. And nothing yet to late, for when I come to him,

Hither will he repaire with a sheepes looke full grim,

By plaine force and violence to driue you to yelde.

C. Custance. If ye two bidde me, we will with him pitche a fielde,

I and my maides together.

M. Mery. Let vs see, be bolde.

C. Custance. Ye shall see womens warre.

T. Trusty. That <u>fight</u> wil I behold.

M. Mery. If occasion serue, takyng his parte full brim,

I will strike at you, but the rappe shall light on him.

When we first appeare.

C. Custance. Then will I runne away

As though I were afeard.

T. Trusty. Do you that part wel play

And I will sue for peace.

M. Mery. And I wil set him on.

Then will he looke as fierce as a Cotssold lyon.

T. Trusty. But when gost thou for him?

M. Mery. That do I very nowe.

C. Custance. Ye shal find vs here.

M. Mery. Wel god haue mercy on you. Ex.

T. Trusty. There is no cause of feare, the least boy in the streete:

C. Custance. Nay, the least girle I haue, will make him take his feete.

But hearke, me thinke they make preparation.

T. Trusty. No force, it will be a good recreation.

C. Custance. I will stand within, and steppe forth speedily,

And so make as though I ranne away dreadfully.

Actus. iiij. Scæna. vij.

R. Royster. M. Merygreeke. C. Custance. D. Doughtie. Harpax. Tristram Trusty.

R. Royster.

Owe sirs, keepe your ray, and see your heartes be stoute,

But where be these caitifes, me think they dare not route,

How sayst thou Merygreeke? What doth Kit Custance say?

M. Mery. I am loth to tell you.

R. Royster. Tushe speake man, yea or nay?

M. Mery. Forsooth sir, I haue spoken for you all that I can.

But if ye winne hir, ye must een play the man,

Een to fight it out, ye must a mans heart take.

R. Royster. Yes, they shall know, and thou knowest I haue a stomacke.

[M. Mery.] A stomacke (quod you) yea, as good as ere man had.

R. Royster. I trowe they shall finde and feele that I am a lad.

M. Mery. By this crosse I haue seene you eate your meate as well,

As any that ere I haue seene of or heard tell,

A stomacke quod you? he that will that denie

I know was neuer at dynner in your companie.

R. Royster. Nay, the stomacke of a man it is that I meane.

M. Mery. Nay the stomacke of a horse or a dogge I weene.

R. Royster. Nay a mans stomacke with a weapon meane I.

M. Mery. Ten men can scarce match you with a spoone in a pie.

R. Royster. Nay the stomake of a man to trie in strife.

M. Mery. I neuer sawe your stomacke cloyed yet in my lyfe.

R. Royster. Tushe I meane in strife or fighting to trie.

M. Mery. We shall see how ye will strike nowe being angry.

R. Royster. Haue at thy pate then, and saue thy head if thou may.

M. Mery. Nay then haue at your pate agayne by this day,

R. Royster. Nay thou mayst not strike at me againe in no wise.

M. Mery. I can not in fight make to you suche warrantise:

But as for your foes here let them the bargaine bie.

R. Royster. Nay as for they, shall euery mothers childe die.

And in this my fume a little thing might make me,

To beate downe house and all, and else the deuill take me.

M. Mery. If I were as ye be, by gogs deare mother,

I woulde not leaue one stone vpon an other.

Though she woulde redeeme it with twentie thousand poundes.

R. Royster. It shall be euen so, by his lily woundes.

M. Mery. Bee not at one with hir vpon any amendes.

R. Royster. No though she make to me neuer so many frendes.

Nor if all the worlde for hir woulde vndertake,

No not God hymselfe neither, shal not hir peace make,

On therfore, marche forwarde, soft, stay a whyle yet.

M. Mery. On.

R. Royster. Tary.

M. Mery. Forth.

R. Royster. Back.

M. Mery. On.

R. Royster. Soft. Now forward set.

C. Custance. What businesse haue we here? out alas, alas.

R. Royster. Ha, ha, ha, ha, ha.

73

Dydst thou see that Merygreeke? how afrayde she was?

Dydst thou see how she fledde apace out of my sight?

Ah good sweete Custance I pitie hir by this light.

M. Mery. That tender heart of yours wyll marre altogether,

Thus will ye be turned with waggyng of a fether.

R. Royster. On sirs, keepe your ray.

M. Mery. On forth, while this geare is hot

R. Royster. Soft, the Armes of Caleys, I haue one thing forgot.

M. Mery. What lacke we now?

R. Royster. Retire, or else we be all slain.

M. Mery. Backe for the pashe of God, backe sirs, backe againe.

What is the great mater?

R. Royster. This hastie forth goyng

Had almost brought vs all to vtter vndoing,

It made me forget a thing most necessarie.

M. Mery. Well remembred of a captaine by sainct Marie.

R. Royster. It is a thing must be had.

M. Mery. Let vs haue it then.

R. Royster. But I wote not where nor how.

M. Mery. Then wote not I when.

But what is it?

R. Royster. Of a chiefe thing I am to seeke.

M. Mery. Tut so will ye be, when ye haue studied a weke.

But tell me what it is?

R. Royster. I lacke yet an hedpiece.

M. Mery. The kitchen collocauit, the best hennes to grece,

Runne, fet it Dobinet, and come at once withall,

And bryng with thee my potgunne, hangyng by the wall,

I haue seene your head with it full many a tyme,

Couered as safe as it had bene with a skrine:

And I warrant it saue your head from any stroke,

Except perchaunce to be amased with the smoke:

I warrant your head therwith, except for the mist,

As safe as if it were fast locked vp in a chist:

And loe here our Dobinet commeth with it nowe.

D. Dough. It will couer me to the shoulders well inow.

M. Mery. Let me see it on.

74

R. Royster. In fayth it doth metely well.

M. Mery. There can be no fitter thing. Now ye must vs tell

What to do.

R. Royster. Now forth in ray sirs, and stoppe no more.

M. Mery. Now sainct George to borow, Drum dubbe a dubbe afore.

T. Trusty. What meane you to do sir, committe manslaughter.

R. Royster. To kyll fortie such, is a matter of laughter.

T. Trusty. And who is it sir, whome ye intende thus to spill?

R. Royster. Foolishe Custance here forceth me against my will.

T. Trusty. And is there no meane your extreme wrath to slake,

She shall some amendes vnto your good mashyp make.

R. Royster. I will none amendes.

T. Trusty. Is hir offence so sore?

M. Mery. And he were a loute she coulde haue done no more.

She hath calde him foole, and dressed him like a foole.

Mocked him lyke a foole, vsed him like a foole.

T. Trusty. Well yet the Sheriffe, the Iustice, or Constable,

Hir misdemeanour to punishe might be able.

R. Royster. No sir, I mine owne selfe will in this present cause,

Be Sheriffe, and Iustice, and whole Iudge of the lawes,

This matter to amende, all officers be I shall,

Constable, Bailiffe, Sergeant.

M. Mery. And hangman and all.

T. Trusty. Yet a noble courage, and the hearte of a man.

Should more honour winne by bearyng with a woman.

Therfore take the lawe, and lette hir aunswere therto.

R. Royster. Merygreeke, the best way were euen so to do.

What honour should it be with a woman to fight?

M. Mery. And what then, will ye thus forgo and lese your right?

R. Royster. Nay, I will take the lawe on hir withouten grace.

75

T. Trusty. Or yf your mashyp coulde pardon this one trespace.

I pray you forgiue hir.

R. Royster. Hoh?

M. Mery. Tushe tushe sir do not.

Be good maister to hir.

R. Royster. Hoh?

M. Mery. Tush I say do not.

And what shall your people here returne streight home?

T. Trustie. Yea, leuie the campe sirs, and hence againe eche one,

R. Royster. But be still in readinesse if I happe to call,

I can not tell what sodaine chaunce may befall.

M. Mery. Do not off your harnesse sirs I you aduise,

At the least for this fortnight in no maner wise,

Perchaunce in an houre when all ye thinke least,

Our maisters appetite to fight will be best.

But soft, ere ye go, haue once at Custance house.

R. Royster. Soft, what wilt thou do?

M. Mery. Once discharge my harquebouse

And for my heartes ease, haue once more with my potgoon.

R. Royster. Holde thy handes else is all our purpose cleane fordoone.

M. Mery. And it cost me my life.

R. Royster. I say thou shalt not.

M. Mery. By the matte but I will. Haue once more with haile shot.

I will haue some penyworth, I will not leese all.

Actus. iiij. Scæna. viij.

Roister Doister

M. Merygreeke. C. Custance. R. Roister. Tib. T. An. Alyface. M. Mumblecrust. Trupenie. Dobinet Doughtie. Harpax. Two drummes with their Ensignes.

C. Custance.

Hat caitifes are those that so shake my house wall?

M. Mery. Ah sirrha now Custance if ye had so muche wit

I woulde see you aske pardon, and your selues submit.

C. Custance. Haue I still this adoe with a couple of fooles?

M. Mery. Here ye what she saith?

C. Custance. Maidens come forth with your tooles.

R. Royster. In a ray.

M. Mery. Dubba dub sirrha.

R. Royster. In a ray.

They come sodainly on vs.

M. Mery. Dubbadub.

R. Royster. In a ray.

That euer I was borne, we are taken tardie.

M. Mery. Now sirs, quite our selues like tall men and hardie.

C. Custance. On afore Truepenie, holde thyne owne Annot,

On towarde them Tibet, for scape vs they can not.

Come forth Madge Mumblecrust, so stande fast togither.

M. Mery. God sende vs a faire day.

R. Royster. See they marche on hither.

Tib. Talk. But mistresse.

C. Custance. What sayst you?

Tib. Shall I go fet our goose?

C. Custance. What to do?

Tib. To yonder Captain I will turne hir loose

And she gape and hisse at him, as she doth at me,

I durst ieoparde my hande she wyll make him flee.

C. Custance. On forward.

R. Royster. They com.

M. Mery. Stand.

R. Royster. Hold.

M. Mery. Kepe.

R. Royster. There.

M. Mery. Strike.

R. Royster. Take heede.

C. Custance. Wel sayd Truepeny.

Trupeny. Ah whooresons.

C. Custance. Wel don in deede

M. Mery. Hold thine owne *Harpax*, downe with them Dobinet.

77

C. Custance. Now Madge, there Annot: now sticke them Tibet.

Tib. Talk. All my chiefe quarell is to this same litle knaue,

That begyled me last day, nothyng shall him saue.

D. Dough. Downe with this litle queane, that hath at me such spite,

Saue you from hir maister, it is a very sprite.

C. Custance. I my selfe will mounsire graunde captaine vndertake,

R. Royster. They win grounde.

M. Mery. Saue your selfe sir, for gods sake.

R. Royster. Out, alas, I am slaine, helpe.

M. Mery. Saue your self.

R. Royster. Alas.

M. Mery. Nay then, haue at you mistresse.

R. Royster. Thou hittest me, alas.

M. Mery. I wil strike at Custance here.

R. Royster. Thou hittest me.

M. Mery. So I wil.

Nay mistresse Custance.

R. Royster. Alas, thou hittest me still.

Hold.

M. Mery. Saue your self sir.

R. Royster. Help, out alas I am slain

M. Mery. Truce, hold your hands, truce for a pissing while or twaine:

Nay how say you Custance, for sauing of your life,

Will ye yelde and graunt to be this gentmans wife?

C. Custance. Ye tolde me he loued me, call ye this loue?

M. Mery. He loued a while euen like a turtle doue.

C. Custance. Gay loue God saue it, so soone hotte, so soone colde,

M. Mery. I am sory for you: he could loue you yet so he coulde.

R. Royster. Nay by cocks precious she shall be none of mine.

M. Mery. Why so?

R. Royster. Come away, by the matte she is man-kine.

I durst aduenture the losse of my right hande,

If shee dyd not slee hir other husbande:

And see if she prepare not againe to fight.

M. Mery. What then? sainct George to borow, our Ladies knight.

R. Royster. Slee else whom she will, by gog she shall not slee mee.

M. Mery. How then?

R. Royster. Rather than to be slaine, I will flee.

C. Custance. Too it againe, my knightesses, downe with them all.

R. Royster. Away, away, away, she will else kyll vs all.

M. Mery. Nay sticke to it, like an hardie man and a tall.

R. Royster. Oh bones, thou hittest me. Away, or else die we shall.

M. Mery. Away for the pashe of our sweete Lord Iesus Christ.

C. Custance. Away loute and lubber, or I shall be thy priest. Exeant om.

So this fielde is ours we haue driuen them all away.

Tib Talk. Thankes to God mistresse, ye haue had a faire day.

C. Custance. Well nowe goe ye in, and make your selfe some good cheere.

Omnes pariter. We goe.

T. Trust. Ah sir, what a field we haue had heere.

C. Custance. Friend Tristram, I pray you be a witnesse with me.

T. Trusty. Dame Custance, I shall depose for your honestie,

And nowe fare ye well, except some thing else ye wolde.

C. Custance. Not now, but when I nede to sende I will be bolde. Exeat.

I thanke you for these paines. And now I wyll get me in,

Now Roister Doister will no more wowyng begin. Ex.

Actus. v. Scæna. j.

Gawyn Goodlucke. Sym Suresby.

Ym Suresby my trustie man, nowe aduise thee well,

And see that no false surmises thou me tell,

Was there such adoe about Custance of a truth?

Sim. Sure. To reporte that I hearde and sawe, to me is ruth,

But both my duetie and name and propretie,

Warneth me to you to shewe fidelitie,

It may be well enough, and I wyshe it so to be,

She may hir selfe discharge and trie hir honestie,

Yet their clayme to hir me thought was very large,

For with letters rings and tokens, they dyd hir charge.

Which when I hearde and sawe I would none to you bring.

G. Goodl. No, by sainct Marie, I allowe thee in that thing.

Ah sirra, nowe I see truthe in the prouerbe olde,

All things that shineth is not by and by pure golde,

If any doe lyue a woman of honestie,

I would haue sworne Christian Custance had bene shee.

Sim. Sure. Sir, though I to you be a seruant true and iust,

Yet doe not ye therfore your faithfull spouse mystrust.

But examine the matter, and if ye shall it finde,

To be all well, be not ye for my wordes vnkinde.

G. Goodl. I shall do that is right, and as I see cause why.

But here commeth Custance forth, we shal know by and by.

Actus. v. Scæna. ij.

C. Custance. Gawyn Goodlucke. Sym Suresby.

C. Custance.

I come forth to see and hearken for newes good,

For about this houre is the tyme of likelyhood,

That Gawyn Goodlucke by the sayings of Suresby,

Would be at home, and lo yond I see hym I.

What Gawyn Goodlucke, the onely hope of my life,

Welcome home, and kysse me your true espoused wife.

Ga. Good. Nay soft dame Custance, I must first by your licence,

See whether all things be cleere in your conscience,

I heare of your doings to me very straunge.

C. Custance. What feare ye? that my faith towardes you should chaunge?

Ga. Good. I must needes mistrust ye be elsewhere entangled.

For I heare that certaine men with you haue wrangled

About the promise of mariage by you to them made.

C. Custance. Coulde any mans reporte your minde therein persuade?

Ga. Good. Well, ye must therin declare your selfe to stande cleere,

Else I and you dame Custance may not ioyne this yere.

C. Custance. Then woulde I were dead, and faire layd in my graue,

Ah Suresby, is this the honestie that ye haue?

To hurt me with your report, not knowyng the thing.

Sim Sure. If ye be honest my wordes can hurte you nothing.

But what I hearde and sawe, I might not but report.

C. Custance. Ah Lorde, helpe poore widowes, destitute of comfort.

Truly most deare spouse, nought was done but for pastance.

G. Good. But such kynde of sporting is homely daliance.

C. Custance. If ye knewe the truthe, ye would take all in good parte.

Ga. Good. By your leaue I am not halfe well skilled in that arte.

81

C. Custance. It was none but Roister Doister that foolishe mome.

Ga. Good. Yea Custance, better (they say) a badde scuse than none.

C. Custance. Why Tristram Trustie sir, your true and faithfull frende,

Was priuie bothe to the beginning and the ende.

Let him be the Iudge, and for me testifie.

Ga. Good. I will the more credite that he shall verifie,

And bicause I will the truthe know een as it is,

I will to him my selfe, and know all without misse.

Come on Sym Suresby, that before my friend thou may

Auouch the same wordes, which thou dydst to me say. Exeant.

Actus. v. Scæna. iij.

Christian Custance.

C. Custance.

O Lorde, howe necessarie it is nowe of dayes,

That eche bodie liue vprightly all maner wayes,

For lette neuer so little a gappe be open,

And be sure of this, the worst shall be spoken

Howe innocent stande I in this for deede or thought?

And yet see what mistrust towardes me it hath wrought

But thou Lorde knowest all folkes thoughts and eke intents

And thou arte the deliuerer of all innocentes.

Thou didst helpe the aduoutresse that she might be amended,

Much more then helpe Lorde, that neuer yll intended.

Thou didst helpe *Susanna*, wrongfully accused,

And no lesse dost thou see Lorde, how I am now abused,

Thou didst helpe *Hester*, when she should haue died,

Helpe also good Lorde, that my truth may be tried.

Yet if Gawin Goodlucke with Tristram Trusty speake,

I trust of yll report the force shall be but weake,

And loe yond they come sadly talking togither,

I wyll abyde, and not shrinke for their comming hither.

Actus. v. Scæna. iiij.

Gawyn Goodlucke. Tristram Trustie. C. Custance. Sym Suresby.

Ga. Good.

And was it none other than ye to me reporte?

Tristram. No, and here were ye wished to haue seene the sporte.

Ga. Good. Woulde I had, rather than halfe of that in my purse.

Sim Sure. And I doe muche reioyce the matter was no wurse,

And like as to open it, I was to you faithfull,

So of dame Custance honest truth I am ioyfull.

For God forfende that I shoulde hurt hir by false reporte.

Ga. Good. Well, I will no longer holde hir in discomforte.

C. Custance. Nowe come they hitherwarde, I trust all shall be well.

Ga. Good. Sweete Custance neither heart can thinke nor tongue tell,

Howe much I ioy in your constant fidelitie,

Come nowe kisse me the pearle of perfect honestie.

C. Custance. God lette me no longer to continue in lyfe,

Than I shall towardes you continue a true wyfe.

Ga. Good. Well now to make you for this some parte of amendes,

I shall desire first you, and then suche of our frendes,

As shall to you seeme best, to suppe at home with me,

Where at your fought fielde we shall laugh and mery be.

Sim Sure. And mistresse I beseech you, take with me no greefe,

I did a true mans part, not wishyng you repreefe.

C. Custance. Though hastie reportes through surmises growyng,

May of poore innocentes be vtter ouerthrowyng,

Yet bicause to thy maister thou hast a true hart,

And I know mine owne truth, I forgiue thee for my part.

Ga. Goodl. Go we all to my house, and of this geare no more.

Goe prepare all things Sym Suresby, hence, runne afore.

Sim Sure. I goe. Ex.

G. Good. But who commeth yond, M. Merygreeke?

C. Custance. Roister Doisters champion, I shrewe his best cheeke.

T. Trusty. Roister Doister selfe your wower is with hym too.

Surely some thing there is with vs they haue to doe.

Actus. v. Scæna. v.

M. Merygreeke. Ralph Roister. Gawyn Goodlucke. Tristram Trustie. C. Custance.

M. Mery.

Ond I see Gawyn Goodlucke, to whome lyeth my message,

I will first salute him after his long voyage,

And then make all thing well concerning your behalfe.

R. Royster. Yea for the pashe of God.

M. Mery. Hence out of sight ye calfe,

Till I haue spoke with them, and then I will you fet,

R. Royster. In Gods name.

M. Mery. What master Gawin Goodluck wel met

And from your long voyage I bid you right welcome home.

Ga. Good. I thanke you.

M. Mery. I come to you from an honest mome.

Ga. Good. Who is that?

M. Mery. Roister Doister that doughtie kite.

C. Custance. Fye, I can scarce abide ye shoulde his name recite.

M. Mery. Ye must take him to fauour, and pardon all past,

He heareth of your returne, and is full yll agast.

Ga. Good. I am ryght well content he haue with vs some chere.

C. Custance. Fye vpon him beast, then wyll not I be there.

Ga. Good. Why Custance do ye hate hym more than ye loue me?

84

C. Custance. But for your mynde sir, where he were would I not be?

T. Trusty. He woulde make vs al laugh.

M. Mery. Ye nere had better sport.

Ga. Good. I pray you sweete Custance, let him to vs resort.

C. Custance. To your will I assent.

M. Mery. Why, suche a foole it is,

As no man for good pastime would forgoe or misse.

Ga. Good. Fet him to go wyth vs.

M. Mery. He will be a glad man. Ex.

T. Trusty. We must to make vs mirth, maintaine hym all we can.

And loe yond he commeth and Merygreeke with him.

C. Custance. At his first entrance ye shall see I wyll him trim.

But first let vs hearken the gentlemans wise talke.

T. Trusty. I pray you marke if euer ye sawe crane so stalke.

Actus. v. Scæna. vj.

R. Roister. M. Merygreeke. C. Custance. G. Goodlucke. T. Trustie. D. Doughtie. Harpax.

R. Royster.

Ay I then be bolde?

M. Mery. I warrant you on my worde,

They say they shall be sicke, but ye be at theyr borde.

R. Royster. Thei wer not angry then.

M. Mery. Yes at first, and made strange

But when I sayd your anger to fauour shoulde change,

And therewith had commended you accordingly,

They were all in loue with your mashyp by and by.

And cried you mercy that they had done you wrong.

R. Royster. For why, no man, woman, nor childe can hate me long.

M. Mery. We feare (quod they) he will be auenged one day,

Then for a peny giue all our liues we may.

R Royster. Sayd they so in deede.

M. Mery. Did they? yea, euen with one voice

85

He will forgiue all (quod I) Oh how they did reioyce.

R Royster. Ha, ha, ha.

M. Mery. Goe fette hym (say they) while he is in good moode,

For haue his anger who lust, we will not by the Roode.

R. Royster. I pray God that it be all true, that thou hast me tolde,

And that she fight no more.

M. Mery. I warrant you, be bolde

Too them, and salute them.

R. Royster. Sirs, I greete you all well.

Omnes. Your maistership is welcom.

C. Custance. Sauyng my quarell.

For sure I will put you vp into the Eschequer.

M. Mery. Why so? better nay: Wherfore?

C. Custance. For an vsurer.

R. Royster. I am no vsurer good mistresse by his armes.

M. Mery. When tooke he gaine of money to any mans harmes?

C. Custance. Yes, a fowle vsurer he is, ye shall see els.

R. Royster. Didst not thou promise she would picke no mo quarels?

C. Custance. He will lende no blowes, but he haue in recompence

Fiftene for one, whiche is to muche of conscience.

R. Royster. Ah dame, by the aunciect lawe of armes, a man

Hath no honour to <u>foile</u> his handes on a woman.

C. Custance. And where other vsurers take their gaines yerely,

This man is angry but he haue his by and by.

Ga. Goodl. Sir, doe not for hir sake beare me your displeasure.

M. Mery. Well, he shall with you talke therof more at leasure.

Vpon your good vsage, he will now shake your hande.

R. Royster. And much heartily welcome from a straunge lande.

M. Mery. Be not afearde Gawyn to let him shake your fyst.

Ga. Goodl. Oh the moste honeste gentleman that ere I wist.

I beseeche your mashyp to take payne to suppe with vs.

M. Mery. He shall not say you nay and I too, by Iesus.

86

Bicause ye shall be friends, and let all quarels passe.

R. Royster. I wyll be as good friends with them as ere I was.

M. Mery. Then let me fet your quier that we may haue a song.

R. Royster. Goe.

G. Goodluck. I haue hearde no melodie all this yeare long.

M. Mery. Come on sirs quickly.

R. Royster. Sing on sirs, for my frends sake.

D. Dough. Cal ye these your frends?

R. Royster. Sing on, and no mo words make.

Here they sing.

Ga. Good. The Lord preserue our most noble Queene of renowne,

And hir virtues rewarde with the heauenly crowne.

C. Custance. The Lorde strengthen hir most excellent Maiestie,

Long to reigne ouer vs in all prosperitie.

T. Trusty. That hir godly proceedings the faith to defende,

He may stablishe and maintaine through to the ende.

M. Mery. God graunt hir as she doth, the Gospell to protect,

Learning and vertue to aduaunce, and vice to correct.

R. Royster. God graunt hir louyng subiects both the minde and grace,

Hir most godly procedyngs worthily to imbrace.

Harpax. Hir highnesse most worthy counsellers God prosper,

With honour and loue of all men to minister.

Omnes. God graunt the nobilitie hir to serue and loue,

With all the whole commontie as doth them behoue.

AMEN.

Certaine Songs to be song by

those which shall vse this Comedie or Enterlude.

The Seconde Song.

Ho so to marry a minion Wyfe,

Hath hadde good chaunce and happe,

Must loue hir and cherishe hir all his life,

And dandle hir in his lappe.

87

If she will fare well, yf she wyll go gay,

A good husbande euer styll,

What euer she lust to doe, or to say,

Must lette hir haue hir owne will.

About what affaires so euer he goe,

He must shewe hir all his mynde,

None of hys counsell she may be kept free,

Else is he a man vnkynde.

The fourth Song.

I mun be maried a Sunday

I mun be maried a Sunday,

Who soeuer shall come that way,

I mun be maried a Sunday.

Royster Doyster is my name,

Royster Doyster is my name,

A lustie brute I am the same,

I mun be maried a Sunday.

Christian Custance haue I founde,

Christian Custance haue I founde,

A Wydowe worthe a thousande pounde,

I mun be maried a sunday.

Custance is as sweete as honey,

Custance is as sweete as honey,

I hir lambe and she my coney,

I mun be maried a Sunday.

When we shall make our weddyng feast,

When we shall make oure weddyng feast,

There shall bee cheere for man and beast,

I mun be maried a Sunday.

I mun be maried a Sunday, etc.

The Psalmodie

Lacebo dilexi,

Maister Roister Doister wil streight go home and die,

Our Lorde Iesus Christ his soule haue mercie vpon:

Thus you see to day a man, to morrow Iohn.

88

Yet sauing for a womans extreeme crueltie,

He might haue lyued yet a moneth or two or three,

But in spite of Custance which hath him weried,

His mashyp shall be worshipfully buried.

And while some piece of his soule is yet hym within,

Some parte of his funeralls let vs here beginne.

Dirige. He will go darklyng to his graue.

Neque lux, neque crux, nisi solum clinke,

Neuer gentman so went toward heauen I thinke.

Yet sirs as ye wyll the blisse of heauen win,

When he commeth to the graue lay hym softly in,

And all men take heede by this one Gentleman,

How you sette your loue vpon an vnkinde woman:

For these women be all suche madde pieuish elues,

They wyll not be woonne except it please them selues.

But in faith Custance if euer ye come in hell,

Maister Roister Doister shall serue you as well.

Good night Roger olde knaue, Farewel Roger olde knaue.

Good night Roger olde knaue, knaue, knap.

Nequando.   Audiui vocem.   Requiem æternam.

Roister Doister

The Peale of belles rong by the parish Clerk,
and Roister Doisters foure men.

The first Bell a Triple.
When dyed he? When dyed he?

The seconde.
We haue hym, We haue hym.

The thirde
Royster Doyster, Royster Doyster.

The fourth Bell.
He commeth, He commeth.

The greate Bell.
Our owne, Our owne.

FINIS.

Made in the USA
Columbia, SC
11 October 2020